MW00584406

Face the Music

Mark Towse

ALL THINGS

THAT MATTER
PRESS

Face the Music
Copyright © 2020 by Mark Towse

All rights reserved. No part of this book may be reproduced or transmitted in any form or by any means without written permission of the author and publisher.

ISBN: 978-1-7334448-7-3
Library of Congress Control Number: 2020930101

Cover art by: Don Noble, Rooster Republic Press

Published in 2020 by All Things That Matter Press

A Low Spirit was previously published in Gallows Hill Print Magazine

Hugh's Friend was previously published Book 'N Pieces and online for Twenty-Two Twenty-Eight Multimedia

Monica Thompson has been included in two anthologies

A Sense of Dread was previously published in Montreal Writes and was produced on The No Sleep Podcast

She's Dead was previously published in Twenty-Two Twenty-Eight, Raconteur

Thorns was previously published in Page and Spine

Stick or Twist was previously published in The Horror Zine

Child was previously published in Montreal Writes

Five Years was previously published in Antipodean SF

The Paperboy was previously published in Gallows Hill and Weird Darkness

The Devil and the Deep Blue Sea was previously published in Centropic Oracle

The Finishing Line was previously published in Weird Darkness

Number Seventy-Two was previously published in Flash Fiction Magazine

I am dedicating this debut collection to my wife, Stephanie, for putting up with my manic mumblings, restless legs, and twisted mind. Incredibly supportive for me to take this path, I cannot thank her enough. A quick mention also for my two children, Adam and Sophie — thanks for discussing your darkest fears with me.

Acknowledgements

For initial editing and feedback, I would like to give a big shout out to my awesome mum, Jennifer Syder. Also, thanks to my dad, Michael Towse, for passing on a twisted sense of humour and raising a son with a unique perspective on the world. Special thanks also go out to Jacqui Wellink, Peter Weymouth, Bob Morton, Loren Dolphin, Deborah Telford, Katherine Towse, Patrick Syder, Paul Foxcroft, and all my readers and supporters that spend their time in my warped little mind.

Thanks to Don Noble, Rooster Republic Press, for a kick-ass cover.

Finally, a big shout out to Deb Harris, All Things That Matter Press, for believing in my work and putting up with this very naive writer.

Table of Contents

A Low Spirit

Under the moonlight, the raven's feathers gleam like fresh paintwork. It watches curiously as my hands claw at the ground. I am getting nowhere. A single tear spills down my cheek, and the cool breeze accentuates its path, but it never makes it to the earth beneath.

I only have myself to blame.

The bird lifts its head; its beady eyes offer no consolation for my guilt. I sit back on the damp ground and reflect on how it came to this.

She used to be so good with the children. It's hard to watch them struggle and hurt in the way they do. Lucy is having nightmares again, and the words I offer do little to comfort. She's always been a worrier, asking questions that should never be on a young child's mind: "Do you still love Mummy?" "Why do you get sad?" "Why does Mummy cry sometimes?"

It's Tom that I worry about most, though. He is not talking at all. I walked in on him a few days ago and caught him crying into his pillow. On his drawing pad on the bedside table there was a picture of the four of us holding hands and smiling.

I feel helpless, even more so here in the middle of the cemetery when I should be at home with the children. I bid farewell to the raven perched atop the stonework and set off home.

I want her back. I want to hold her and have another go at making her happy. We used to be.

The first time I saw her, I knew I wanted to be with her—intelligent, altruistic, complex, generous, and very stubborn—my ever so stubborn English Rose. I loved her.

Our friends were shocked at how we would speak to each other at times, but I don't think they ever truly understood how comfortable we felt in each other's presence. We would joke and roast like best friends, love like adulterers, and talk all night about anything under the sun. That seems like such a long time ago now.

A streetlight casts its warm glow on our house, but inside the light dwindles and only makes it up the first three steps of the staircase. I creep up the boards slowly, half expecting a loud creak and subsequent cry from Lucy, but the house remains mute.

I pass the photo on the wall that portrays a lie. It's a recent one of Anne on her fortieth, trying to smile as though she'd forgotten how. Depression had finally rooted itself. Pangs of guilt wash over me again as I run my finger over her forced smile. The make-up helps disguise the sleepless nights and taut face, but the eyes offer nothing but despondence.

The isolation was unbearable, and I know that comes across as selfish, but I was trying to hold everything together. After a while, I felt the cracks appear. My work was suffering, I was snappy at Lucy and Tom, and I used to get so frustrated with Anne. On occasions, I felt so rigid with rage I feared what might happen. Those times I would drive to the beach and cry or scream — or both.

She seemed so adamant on self-destruction. I tried, but there is only so much I could do on my own. Admittedly, I was afraid to tap into that part of her mind. It would be like trying to defuse a bomb and if you didn't know which wires to cut … boom!

She had battled waves of it over the years. Sometimes it would last days and sometimes weeks, but she had always managed to fight her way out in the end. It was exhausting for both of us, and I couldn't help but feel that sometimes I made it worse. I used to think perhaps if she was with someone else, they could help her unlock the unshakable sadness that I couldn't.

My patience grew thin over time, and I shamefully started to throw around desperate ultimatums, threatening to leave and to take the kids. I couldn't reach her. She would happily take the drugs, but not the advice, and the pills she had started taking encouraged even more disconnect.

Gently, I stroke Lucy's cheek. She looks peaceful now, and I hope some light is getting through to her dreams. I want to scoop her up and squeeze her. She kept me going through a lot of the hard times, and I feel as though I have let her down, too.

I peek into Tom's room and see the drawing of the four of us still on his table. He's curled up in a ball as though in self-protection mode and he looks so small and vulnerable. I want to wake him up and tell him everything is going to be okay. I kiss him on the forehead and whisper I love him before moving to our room.

I wanted a happy ending, back to where we used to be. I begged her countless times to see someone.

I had nothing left to give at the end.

The dresser that used to be packed to the brim with bottles of colourful tablets is now almost empty apart from the ripped open envelope and letter cast aside. I have read that first line so many times now.

Dear Mrs. Jones

This is to confirm your booking with psychologist Dr. Lauper on 17th September at 10 am.

There is a small groan behind me, and I turn to look at my wife in bed and watch her until she settles once again.

The envelope is postmarked the 4th September, the day before I locked myself in the garage with the engine running. She never said a word. Maybe she was frightened of failure.

I will never forgive myself. The raven has watched me helplessly claw at my grave many times—punishment enough, perhaps.

Hugh's Friend

When I speak to my friends, we often joke and reminisce about the past. One such time we got to speaking about the imaginary friends we used to have as kids and how we would often play or discuss things with them and even argue with them; perhaps it was just an instinctive way of preparing ourselves for growing up.

The general rule of thumb was they would come out on request—when you wanted to play or just not be alone. My imaginary friend was called Hugh. He was two years older than me, was an exception to the rule, and I used to think he was a prick.

We were sitting at the dinner table one day and, as my mum was reaching for the veggies, he slipped under the table and came back up, holding his nose and gagging, before telling me that my mum wasn't wearing any knickers. He also said he caught my dad playing with himself in the shower earlier and he wasn't goddamn surprised. I intentionally dropped my fork to prove he was telling tales. That vision still haunts me today.

Some things he told me were truths, and others were just outright lies designed to ruin self-confidence and push anxiety levels through the roof. Hugh found this taunting to be hilarious. For example, on my seventh birthday, he told me I was adopted, and the papers were in the third drawer down of my mum's dresser. All I found was a bunch of knickers and bras and what looked to be a torch that vibrated. Hugh told me that my Mum used to shove the torch so far up her 'doodaa' you could see her tonsils. Obviously, I didn't believe him. He lied about the adoption and the torch, and he was full of shit.

At that point, he also told me that my mum was sleeping with the postman and that my dad was a serial killer. Hugh said he could prove it, but I'd had enough. I actually tried to unimagine him from my mind for a good couple of weeks before I realised the stubborn little jerk wasn't going anywhere.

The first day at school, already a hard enough time for a seven-year-old, was something I will never forget. The teacher placed me next to some kid called Robert. He seemed nice enough, but Hugh seemed almost jealous that I had even said hello to him.

In my ear all day: "Jack has a boyfriend. Jack has a boyfriend," and, slightly more inventive, "Jack and Bobby sitting in a tree, Jack blows Bobby, one-two-three."

That carried on all day until I lost the plot and screamed at the top of my lungs in front of the entire classroom, "I don't have a fucking boyfriend!"

Some kids laughed, some went white. The teacher did neither, but did escort me from the class.

Mum picked me up early that day. She was very disappointed, to say the least. Hugh, however, was still unbelievably pleased with himself. When we got back to the house, he asked me to follow him as he had something that he wanted to show me.

"Where are we going?" I called out to him in pursuit as he sprinted ahead down the hallway and towards the back end of the house.

"You'll see soon enough," he replied as he finally made it to the cellar door.

My dad always said the cellar was a work in progress and too dangerous for us to go in. I always wondered why it didn't apply to him, though.

"Hugh, I'm not allowed in there, even Mum isn't."

"Do you ever think to yourself why not?" he asked as he pointed to a jar on top of the cupboard. I grabbed the key from it and unlocked the door. The air conditioner was already on and I still recall the cool blast from the room as I opened the door. I remember a lot about that day. I flicked the light switch on, and nothing happened. "Oh, yes, in the cupboard next to the door," Hugh said. And I went back and grabbed the torch. As I felt my way along the walls, I saw the vast array of jars and bottles of wine spread across various tables.

"What are we doing here, Hugh?" I asked impatiently.

"Keep going, nearly there," he replied.

I kept edging along the wall and finally came to the end of the room. I flashed the torch around and could see nothing else worth noting.

"Push that last panel, Jack," he said.

I did, and it moved inwards not just a little bit. I soon realised it was a makeshift door.

"How do you know all this?"

"Go inside, Jack."

I stepped inside and swept the torch around, then shrieked and dropped it. I scrambled on the floor in a mix of fear and panic and finally felt the handle and pointed it forwards again. The little boy covered his eyes, and I moved the torch to the left, out of his direct line of sight. As he cowered in the corner, I noticed the chain attached to the bolt in the floor and a plate and glass on the mattress next to him.

"This is Peter," Hugh said very casually.

"Why are you in our house, Peter?" I asked.

Peter didn't say anything. He sat shaking.

"You need to ask your dad," Hugh stated.

As I turned around to shine the torch towards Hugh, I saw the etchings on the wooden interior of the room.

Hugh was here.

Monica Thompson

There is a voice in my head telling me not to jump—at least I think it's in my head. It's a soft voice, and very faint, as though coming from a long distance away. I've heard it three days running now.

I can feel a force pulling me back, not fear exactly, but it feels as though something else has me in its grasp. I can see the people below scurrying like ants, oblivious to my existence and pursuing their pointless tasks. I am twenty storeys high, perched on the edge of my apartment building and wondering how it came to this. Not so long ago, I was happy and excited about the future. How quickly the ground can fall from beneath us. I step from the edge and, for the third time this week, I cowardly resign myself to doing it tomorrow and walk back down to my apartment.

It's a warm Sunday evening in the middle of spring, usually my favourite season, but not this year. I open the window, close my eyes, and let the gentle breeze rush over me; I pretend it is her warm breath and that her face is close to mine.

"I miss you, Julie," I say, and the breeze is gone and the illusion fades.

The smell of the street food is wafting through my window, and I am immediately hungry. We would often walk hand in hand on the streets below trying a selection of the foods on offer.

Six long months have passed since she died.

We were so excited to move into this area; a great school if we ever decided to have kids, it was close to our offices, and had more than enough shops and restaurants. Our professions, I as a marketing director and Julie as a lawyer provided a pretty good living here. It felt safe for us, too, a great place to raise a family—until people started dying.

It was a relatively small town with a population of just over five thousand, yet there had been three murders and three tragic accidents in the space of seven months with a death toll of nine. For a small town, that's high. One house fire, two road accidents, and two same-day stabbings. There is an ominous feeling around town, a dangerous cocktail of paranoia and uncertainty. I see the For Sale signs going up everywhere, and there seems to be a real urgency for people to get out. They must sense the menace in the air as I do.

The news had said the two stabbings were carried out by someone with a sick mind. A middle-aged man named Peter Whyte had subsequently been committed to a psychiatric hospital. It had shown interviews with people that knew Peter, and the consensus was that up until his wife's accident three months ago he'd been a stand-up guy, headmaster at the local secondary school, with no history of violence or mental illness.

Amidst all the chaos, the thought of leaving town has never crossed my mind; I feel as though I would be deserting Julie. This is our home. The photograph on the table shows us at the fun fair, our faces covered with candy floss and Julie's makeshift pink beard. I just can't let go of her. How could I let go of anyone I loved so deeply?

As I pick up the photo frame, an image suddenly invades my melancholy. I recognise my wife's office. Sitting across from her are two people that I don't know: a pretty but tired-looking red headed lady with an old bruise plastered across her right eye, and next to her a smug looking teenager. I try and look for some other details, but I'm instantly pulled back into our living room and left staring at the pictured document of happier times.

Julie?

The phone rings and brings me back; it's John, my boss. The conversation is short. He wants to see me in his office tomorrow. He's been fair, but people expect you to get over it eventually. It is quite savage really. How can anyone possibly carry on as usual?

I still think I see her from time to time. I know it's my mind playing tricks on me, but I go along for the ride. It can't be her as her body was almost cut in two and it took the emergency services three hours to pull her from the wreckage. The woman who collided into her said she'd swerved to avoid a woman standing in the middle of the road, but no witnesses saw anyone, only her car slamming into our car and my wife veering off into the ditch. She wasn't over the limit, passed a drug test, and she didn't even have her phone on her at the time. The judge saw no reason to punish her. I can't forgive her, though. Her story doesn't add up and, right or wrong, I still feel resentment that she's alive and Julie isn't.

I can't face going into the office tomorrow. I don't need to hear the "we have given you enough time" bullshit.

I've made my mind up that I will definitely jump. I want to see Julie again. I appreciate how selfish that may seem, and I will leave loved ones behind, but I feel I'm in limbo, and I can't shake it. I stand by the decision.

After turning on the television and skipping a few programmes that Julie and I may have previously watched but now just seem like noise, I end up on the news channel. The breaking news talks about another murder, a young man named Chris Beckworth found in a rubbish bin.

It was another shooting at point-blank range; one shot to the head. The reporter mentions they have the person responsible in custody and expect to make a full statement shortly.

My parents call and I tell them I'm fine. They've been awesome and were there when I needed them most. Now it all seems so overbearing as they're trying to force me back into the real world, asking how work is, am I eating enough, and, worst of all, am I dating.

I put on my shoes and jacket and start walking the same path that Julie and I have travelled many times. We always held hands, and I extend mine now and imagine she's walking next to me. The sensation stuns me; I can feel warmth extend across my palm, as though she has slotted her hand in mine. A cyclist passes and looks back, and I realise I must look odd, but I am not prepared to let this feeling go. I keep my arm and hand extended. I sit on our bench and again close my eyes as the warm air blows through. There's a tickle on my cheek; I imagine her dark hair falling across my face. The wind stops and again she is gone. I look around and notice the park is much quieter than it used to be. The events have cast a shadow over the town, and it will most likely never be the same again.

I return home and then drive to the supermarket, another chore that we'd share and is all the more painful because of that. I fill my basket with fruit and vegetables and spot some people I know. I don't want to go through the charade again. As I rush to the next aisle, I knock some poor lady flying to the floor.

"I'm sorry, are you okay?" I ask.

She's looking at me but not saying anything, and we stay in awkward silence for a while before I finally offer my apologies again. I reach for her and grab her arm to help her up and a scene plays in my head. I'm behind the wheel of a car. I look to the left and see my wife on the other lane of the freeway and I hear a voice say "bitch," and I turn the wheel hard left. I am heading straight for my wife's car.

And suddenly I'm back in the supermarket. The woman has pulled her arm free and is running off shouting, "I'm sorry". I chase her into the car park and see the car rolling out, spray job on the front. I run towards it, but all I manage is to brush my hand against one of the windows and then she's gone. I get into my car and pursue her and, after pulling out, see her about eight cars ahead. I follow her for about ten minutes before she turns into Fortescue Street and, after pulling over, watch the green Mercedes eventually come to a halt about a hundred yards away. She gets out the car and rushes into the house. I don't think she realises I followed her. I'm not really sure what my next move should be. The scene replays in my head. How was it possible that

I could see what she saw? Why was I being shown this, and what am I supposed to do with this information?

The voice had said "bitch," making it sound as though the collision was deliberate. There was no sign of a woman standing in the middle of the road in the short movie I'd just witnessed.

What did this woman have against my wife? I need answers to my questions, and I am going to get them.

A man is coming out of the house now and towards my car. I start the engine and he begins to run as I manage to get it into gear and wheel skid away. I head home to try and get my head around what I have seen today, relieved for once to get back to the apartment. I pour a whisky and sit on our couch.

My palms begin to hurt and I realise I'm digging my fingernails into them.

I'd thought I recognised her from somewhere but couldn't make the connection. Now I know. She killed my wife. She's the one that took Julie away from me, and there she was grocery shopping as if nothing had ever happened. How am I supposed to leave it there?

I was supposed to find this information. It's surely Julie's voice in my head that keeps me from jumping and is the invisible restraint I feel that pulls me back. She's sending me a message.

I open up the laptop and trawl through the news. The man in custody has confessed to the murder of Chris Beckworth this morning. He said the victim was sleeping with his wife. I note further down that in a brief interview given by the wife that she vehemently denies ever knowing Mr. Beckworth.

They show a picture of Chris alive and smiling on the news site, and I place my cursor over the photo. In an instant, I snap my arm back as a jolt of pain shoots up the bone along with a burst of visuals in my head and images of a hotel room. Chris Beckworth stands next to the hotel window looking down. The scene moves across to the bed, and I see a woman wrapped in sheets. She is crying, and her mascara has started to run. It is unmistakably the same red-haired woman I saw when I picked up the photo frame earlier. The scene melts away, and all that remains is a ringing in my ears and a tingling sensation in my arm.

I won't miss this place. It started out as a little utopia for us, but there is an evil undertone running through it now. I have one last thing to do before I can leave and join my wife. I down my whisky and close my eyes for a while. When I wake up, the light has faded. My watch tells me that three hours have passed.

The shower feels great on my skin, and I close my eyes and let the hot water rush over me. Julie and I had sex in here many times and, unlike the scenes from a movie, it was generally always clumsy and often triggered hysterical laughter. Our buttocks would press against the glass doors and bottles of shampoo or shower gel might fall on our toes, or we would get wrapped up in the shower curtain. Sometimes we'd give up and take it to the bedroom, but the shower holds great memories, and I could quite happily stay here for hours. When I step out and reach for a towel, I see the letters on the bathroom mirror:

Monica.

That must be her name. I'm on my way, Julie. I'm on my way.

I dress and leave my apartment, but not before picking up a knife from the cutlery draw. I don't bother locking my door.

There's an old couple heading up the stairwell; they have no idea I'm about to commit a murder. A normal day in hell town, I think. One of them bumps into me and we both recoil as what feels like an electric shock passes between us. A scene subsequently plays in my head of him driving towards a couple on the path, and I see the woman fly over the bonnet. I recognise Peter Whyte, the ex-headmaster, from the news programme standing dumbfounded on the path, watching the lady come to rest, limbs twisted, in the middle of the road. We part ways after a short but uncomfortable silence, and I can see the guilt he is carrying in his face. He doesn't look like he has slept for weeks.

The warmth has gone now, and there is a slight chill in the air. I shiver intensely and not just because of the cold. I start the engine, turn the heater on, and make my way to Fortescue Street. As I drive down the freeway, I see some wreckage on the side of the road and an ambulance approaching. I can make out a smashed windscreen, and some people standing around a motionless figure near the edge of the road. I pull over to the side and wind the window down, and I recognise Tom, the manager from the local bank, on the ground, covered in blood and unnaturally contorted.

What the hell is going on?

The deaths are getting closer together, and I feel that something big is going to happen soon. It's hard to explain, but there's a malignant and oppressive taste in the air, and it's making me sick to the stomach.

I stop around the corner from Fortescue Street and get out the car. I walk up to the beginning of the road and look towards the house. They're sitting in the garden on the bench at the front wrapped in a blanket and each holding a glass of wine. They're sitting in their front yard drinking wine while Julie rots in the ground. I can hear their laughter now.

The voice enters my head again. It sounds like whispering from some distance away, but I can make out the words kill and hurry. "I'm coming, Julie," I whisper back.

I rush back to the car and start the engine, turning into the road with headlights off; I don't want to give them a warning. I'm forty metres away now. I bring the car to a halt and watch them laugh. I hit the accelerator, the car spins into action, and I'm heading straight for them. Everything feels like it's in slow motion as I see them look up towards the approaching heap of metal, their wine glasses appearing to float down toward the ground as realisation hits and they drop them. Now I am only ten yards away.

"Julie!"

As I see her ahead of me, I turn the steering wheel as hard as I can and hit the brakes. The car spins around and the tyres squeal, and I momentarily catch the terrified eyes of the woman I nearly murdered. I know she understands. The car comes to a halt. My hands are white and clenched around the steering wheel as though they have become one. There are voices—shouting and screaming. I put the car back in first and speed off, heart and head pounding in unison.

I park the car a few blocks away and walk back to the apartment. This gives me time to consider what I'm doing and the obvious hate that has consumed my rationality.

Julie.

I saw her.

She's here with me.

I miss you, Julie.

She didn't want me to kill that lady, and I know she would have never condoned such an act. I used her as an excuse. But what about the voices and the name on the mirror?

At the flat, I pour some whisky, something that is becoming quite habitual, and sit in front of the laptop. I start scrolling through some old news articles. Before recent events, the place had seemed so pleasantly mundane. Ordinary occurrences of a quiet town, stories about local artists and businesses, the local football team, uproar at a new estate they were thinking of building. Then I come across the fire, a single house fire that seems to have set off this domino effect of chaos. The name jumps out at me immediately and sends my mind spinning at a thousand thoughts per minute.

Monica. The name that had appeared in the bathroom mirror.

It was her family that died in the house fire. The name stands out for another reason.

Why?

I search some more under the name and then I see her image. I reach for my whisky, hand trembling towards the glass, and knock it back before looking at the screen again. The monitor displays a picture of a red-headed woman—the one I'd seen in Julie's office when I picked up the photograph earlier, and the one from the vision in the hotel room with Chris Beckworth.

Who was she?

I read some more and find the full name: Monica Thompson.

***

I haven't been in here for months, but I'm in the office and going through Julie's files, looking for old notes that might help give clarity on events. It doesn't take me long to find what I'm looking for. Thompson. I open it up and see the scribbles down the side and the typed text: James Thompson. Drug charge. The notes were directed more towards his mum than the case itself. The word intervention with a question mark was the most noticeable in bold writing. I read further down the page to find out she'd taken this case pro bono as the bank was hassling Monica for repayment of debts. She'd drawn a ring around Monica's name and noted adjacent to it, notes about mood swings, anti-depressants, and facial bruising.

I remember now.

Julie had mentioned James and his mum before. She wasn't one to normally talk about her clients, but this one was a concern. The last few times Julie had seen her, she had been frantic, and always carrying an injury of some sort. On the last visit a few months ago, she'd been manic. James had been expelled, and the prospect of time in prison loomed. She even threatened Julie last time. She'd met someone else, and they were going to make a go of it, but if her son went down, it would spoil everything, and she would hold Julie responsible.

Chris Beckworth.

I had wanted to call the police, but she refused and said the woman needed help, not further problems.

James did end up doing time for the drug offence.

I pour myself another whisky—this is too much information to digest in such a small space of time. There had been a sequence of events that had a common thread: Monica. Too many people have died for this to be a coincidence. Julie, Peter Whyte, Chris Beckworth, Tom, and the other deaths that were more than likely related.

It's all too much. I want to feel Julie's presence again. I know what will bring her to me.

I leave my apartment and head for the top of the building.

Here I am again, standing at the edge. I close my eyes and wait to feel the resistance as I lean over. Instead of pulling me back, this time there's a force that is pushing me forward, and I'm struggling to keep balance as my centre of gravity is thrown.

There is someone trying to push me off.

I feel an energy surge through every part of me, and in a flash of light I find myself back behind the wheel of the lady's car — and this time I see her, Monica, standing in the road. I hear the driver scream and look across to see my wife in the other car. We collide, and the jolt transports me into Monica's house. I am watching her lock all the windows and doors and then she turns the gas knob and lights the match. The subsequent explosion is bone-shaking. I am thrown back into a small room, and Peter Whyte is behind his desk, telling Monica that her son is no longer welcome at the school. I look towards Monica and then back towards Peter, only to find the bank manager instead, and the surrounding office has changed, too. I am standing behind Monica watching her, with her head in her hands, sobbing, and the scene changes again and she is in bed now. I am in the hotel room, the one from my earlier vision, listening to the admission from Chris Beckworth that he will never leave his wife.

I know it has been Monica with me on top of this building and not Julie, the hateful thoughts now pouring from her into me. She wanted me alive so I could play my part in her vendetta.

I am suddenly back, present, but it's too late — my foot slips and I fall but manage to grab the side of the stonework, and I'm hanging now twenty storeys above the cold hard concrete below.

I look up to see Monica's face, a charred and sinewy mess with only a few red hairs remaining on her head.

"Like everyone else, you let me down," she screamed.

This malignant bitch is taking everyone down who had ever wronged her. Her little network of deceit and manipulation is everywhere, and she's out of control.

She smiles a menacing smile, no lips, just a bit of charred skin attached to her jawline and she lifts her bony arms back to give one final push, but not before Julie appears with an arm around her throat dragging her back to the ground. They thrash around on the floor in a violent struggle, and the two of them meld into a cataclysm of good versus evil. The screams pierce the air, and I see Monica burst into flames as the hatred and anger continues to flow through her, and I feel Julie's pain, immediate and intense, and my flesh feels like it's on fire, too.

I can feel Julie's remaining strength surging through my veins, trying to keep me going. She's fighting two battles here. I try to pull myself up, but I don't have it in me, and all I can do is watch this fight for spiritual ascendancy.

Eventually, the two vanish in an explosion of light and my pain is gone.

I am left hanging. I can feel my fingers slipping. There are no footholds to push myself up. I am left only with my thoughts.

Julie tried to give me warnings with the photo, the bathroom, the news article. She's been trying to break through. I've been too obsessed with hate, and that's why it's been so easy for Monica to manipulate me. Monica is the root of all evil in this town and —

Her beautiful face appears from over the edge and her hand extends towards mine.

"Grab my hand," Julie says softly and smiles that smile.

I look her in the eyes and I'm immediately overwhelmed with love.

"I've missed you," I say.

I let go of the edge and drift toward the ground, blissful.

I can't live without her. I don't want to.

I stand by my decision.

Family Tree

"Look at it, Deb," I shout excitedly.

Since an early age, I've always had a fondness for trees. I think it comes down to their stability and hardiness, their stubbornness to give in to the harsh elements.

The tree was a sanctuary for me as a child; somewhere to escape when my parents argued. It was only a few hundred yards away from our house. I remember thinking that its trunk must stretch over a mile towards the sky. The huge roots were a sight, too—like twisted human limbs that had been turned to stone.

"Yes, darling, it really is rather beautiful. Can we move on now?" my wife replies edgily, one hand on her hip.

She'd call it an obsession. And she would probably be right.

During the seemingly endless time spent in the back of my parents' car trying to block out the constant bickering, I looked for the trees that stood out from others—not necessarily the tallest or widest, but ones that suggested importance and non-conformity. Some of them appeared otherworldly to me.

I always insist we never leave the house without the camera. My wife, Deborah, has put up with it for years now, but I think it's started to become a bit of a bore for her. She would describe our house as a wall to wall collage of trees and forests. And this one—this beautiful, gigantic oak tree is the one that takes centre stage in our living room—an eight-foot by six-foot canvas that monopolises the wall.

The tree holds so many memories, and it's the one I have always deemed to be the most majestic of them all. Magical. And as I run my hands along its ancient scaly bark and rest my left cheek against its coarseness, I feel alive and inexplicably whole.

My mum loved this tree, too. We used to call it our mystic tree.

It was under this tree that I proposed to Deb. Packed a picnic basket full of wine and cheese and, in one of the blocks, I concealed the ring. Her face was a picture. It went beyond love making what happened under the tree afterward. It was animalistic—an urgent cocktail of greed, pain, pleasure, and lust, a strange thing to happen for two ordinarily prudish people. And we have never spoken of it since, as though it would detract from the emotional resonance of the commitment we made to each other that day. It's our first time back together, and she is still obviously uncomfortable about what happened. She came with me, though. I will give her that.

I was hoping it might stir up some of that passion again.

I come back alone frequently. There is something sacred about this piece of land that stays with me long after my visits. Sometimes I even see the tree in my dreams, standing proud and basking in the darkness of night. It comes to life: broad limbs snaking against each other, moans of pleasure and pain carrying on the gentle wind that rattles through its leaves. Other times, I think I hear my mother's voice coming from deep within its spine.

When I'm not here, I feel unprotected, vulnerable, and exposed. Now, beneath its tremendous canopy, I feel untouchable. Special. Divine.

And right now, I want to feel that urge again, the one Deb and I had that day.

She's everything to me, but I'm losing her. She's slipping away. We haven't made love for months. And she always seems so distant.

I'm beginning to feel the energy around me. The gentle aromas of earth and wood and the filtered sun against my cheek make the hairs prickle on the back of my neck. As I move in towards her, I reach for her hand and, after gently removing it from her hip, begin to kiss the palm.

"What are you doing, Brian?"

"Come on, Deb. Let's give it a—"

"Brian, I'm leaving you."

And the wind is knocked out of me. Suddenly, I can't get enough air and there's a tightening in my chest—it feels like a knot in my stomach, just like the misshapen base I'm doubled over.

"I've been trying to find the right time."

"Is ... is there someone else?" is all I can think to say.

"What? No. It's not about that, Brian. I just don't think we have anything in common anymore. You don't do anything. Your life revolves around your photography and these goddamned trees!"

"But I—"

"How many times have I asked you to take an interest in what I'm doing? To do something I enjoy? But it's all about you and this unhealthy fixation with these stupid fucking over-sized plants."

The knot is beginning to twist inside my stomach. And as I continue to stare at the serpentine limbs of the tree, they slowly begin to writhe against each other, too.

I can hear her still talking behind me, but I'm not listening to the words. The gentle rustling of the leaves and soft creak of the branches is all I can hear—the soothing music of nature. Sunlight is fading as the network of branches above us bind themselves together.

"Brian!"

I turn to look at her as she begins her retreat.

The moans of the tree can be heard all around as the first branch swoops down behind her and coils around her neck. Her eyes are wide with fear as she frantically begins to claw at the woody limb that is wrapping itself around her throat.

"Help," she tries to scream, but the word is only a raspy gurgle.

My instincts are to go and rescue her, to save the day. Maybe she'd re-evaluate and fall back in love with me. But I know deep down that's just fantasy.

More branches begin to shoot around her midriff, and soon she's being pulled in towards the central trunk. She holds her arms out on the way past, and I immediately lift the camera and take some pictures. Her motion doesn't blur the shots; it's a rather clever piece of equipment, this one. The screaming is slowly drowned out by a series of leaf-filled branches that begin to enter her throat, and I watch with fascination as they slowly work their way down. There is an uneasy sensation as her eyes look at me in disbelief, but it's camera worthy, and I take another shot. Photography is all about the eyes.

Sunlight falls on my face once again as the remaining branches begin to close in around her. When she is brought in against the trunk, the slithering roots become even more active, and I find myself slightly aroused as she slowly starts sinking into the orgy of limbs.

And then she is gone.

Some of the leaves fall to the floor as the tree begins to move in more spasmodic and abrupt movements, like heavy machinery jolting into action. But then it stops.

The branches reach out towards the sky and the shadow of the canopy once again casts its tapestry on the ground below.

It's for the best.

Now we can work on our relationship.

I can devote some proper time to her.

I bring the camera to eye level and take a final snapshot of the tree. There is nothing as beautiful as nature.

"Bye, Deb. I'll be back soon," I say, before kissing the trunk and making my way to the car.

***

The photos come out better than expected. Some of them find their way into my special folder, but that final picture will replace the one in the living room, the one I named Mother Nature.

I still recall the immense feeling of betrayal and sadness when Mum told me she was leaving Dad. That's why she brought us that day to our favourite tree: to tell me the news. She told me that I could come and visit whenever I wanted, but when I asked if I could go with her, she said, no, it wasn't an option. And that's when rage took over. How dare she leave us, abandon us? And that same knot presented itself and began to churn within me. There was screaming, swearing, and name-calling and so many tears, but I could not shake the overwhelming anger. The tree began to move behind her. I wanted to say something but knew I was partly responsible. All I could do was watch as she was drawn into its epicentre and slowly sank into its arms.

She's still on the missing persons' register. I suppose Deb will be on the same list soon.

It's interesting to compare the photographs and the now larger base of limbs. I'm going to call this one Family Tree.

A Sense of Dread

Tom has been waking up the last few days with a sense of dread. Recently experiencing severe bouts of panic, Tom's heartburn has been almost unbearable. Today is no exception. Tom feels that this impending feeling of dread will manifest itself in some shape or form, and it's making him even more anxious than usual.

He leaves the bed and pulls the covers back over his wife, telling her he's going to make coffee. He leans over, turns off the alarm clock, and heads down to the kitchen to grind some beans. He grabs the pestle and mortar from the cupboard, deciding that he needs to alleviate some stress, and starts grinding with an unnecessary ferocity. Most of the coffee spills over onto the floor, so he gives up, unable to cope with the prospect of picking it out from the already dirty tiles. He sighs, grabs the teabags, and shouts, "I've made a small mess, but don't worry, I'll clean it up."

The pots are piled high, so he rinses two dirty cups and fills them with water once the kettle boils. He begins to dip the bag into the first one, but it bursts, so he empties both cups in the kitchen sink and then bends down to spoon the powdered coffee into the filter.

He starts to sob.

Eventually, he gathers himself, pours the coffee, and takes the cups with him through to the hallway and up the dimly lit stairs towards the bedroom. He stops halfway up to look at the picture of him and Judith on the wall, their wedding day, and a snapshot of history when everything was okay—before the accident. He studies the photo as he has done many times—her skin like porcelain and a smile that drew him in from the moment he saw her. She had chrysanthemums in her hair. On the day itself, he thought they were daisies until Judith had laughed and corrected him. His own face, too, was one of genuine happiness; after all, he had just landed the love of his life, and nothing could stop him.

Christ, I love you, Judith.

As he reaches the top of the stairs, he tries to elbow away an annoying bluebottle fly that's buzzing around his head, causing him to spill some of the coffee as he trips over the damned vacuum once again. Tom rushes to the bathroom, puts the coffee on the edge of the tub, and grabs a towel from the rack to wipe himself down. He sighs, leans over and turns both taps, watching her in the large oval mirror as the water rushes in, filling the tub. When it's half full, Tom turns off the water and goes into the bedroom to help his wife out of bed. She's heavier than usual, but Tom doesn't comment. He knows it'll only get him in trouble.

Tom carries Judith into the bathroom and helps lower her into the bath. He asks if the temperature is okay, not bothering to wait for a response as he lights some scented candles and pours in some bubble bath—the lavender one she likes. The colour contrasts nicely with her pale skin.

His mobile phone begins to ring and immediately his pulse quickens. He knows it's his boss—he didn't go in last week and ignored the e-mails. Questions were being asked and it would only be a matter of time before they found out. It had started small, a little bit at a time from a couple of clients, but a few bad bets and he started to get careless.

He lets it go to voicemail.

Tom checks his reflection in the bathroom mirror and, even through the steam, he can make out the sallow skin that frames the large dark circles under his eyes. He's seen better days. His mostly grey hair is matted and unwashed, and he hasn't shaved for nearly a week. He contemplates showering, but the thought of the required effort distresses him, so he splashes some water on his face instead and swallows some toothpaste straight from the tube. His wife recently told him that toothpaste causes cancer. He had laughed at that, pinched his nose, and asked for a kiss. Tom enjoyed the times they fooled around like that.

He walks through to their bedroom, lifts his dressing gown and, for the next few minutes, masturbates furiously—a habit he has picked up over the last few days. Once he's done, he goes back downstairs with his coffee, being careful not to trip over the vacuum. He puts some bread in the toaster and opens the fridge to find he has no margarine left. In fact, there is nothing spreadable at all. He sits and waits for the toast to pop up. Eventually, it does, and even though he prepared himself for the pop, it still startles him, and he estimates his heart rate increases by at least ten beats per minute. He takes the toast and places it on the cleanest plate he can find from the dirty stack, but when he reaches for his coffee, the toast slides from his plate onto the kitchen floor.

He wants to cry again but refrains as he bends over and collects it from the dirty floor and gives it a quick shake. He takes a bite and chews solemnly, washing it down with a swig of his coffee. He stops to pull some hair from his teeth, no doubt gathered from the floor, and then pours the remainder of the coffee down the sink.

Tom looks down at his overhanging belly and suddenly feels the impulse to go for a run. He considers it very seriously for a few seconds before deciding it would be quite an upheaval, so he switches on the television instead. He flicks through the various channels until he finds a nature documentary. Settling into his chair, he begins to pick at his immature beard and pulls out a huge dark hair with the follicle still attached. Tom chews off the follicle and begins to think he's losing his mind.

On TV, a deer is running for its life, closely followed by the jaguar that's hungry for its dinner. Tom changes the channel quickly, suddenly contemplating how savage existence is. He convinces himself that if reincarnation is real, he would no doubt come back as a deer. Or worse, he'd come back as himself.

In his melancholy state, he finds his thoughts wandering back to the early years, before marriage, back when he and his future wife told each other everything. Judith said she once ate a worm when she was nine, and that was pretty much the worst thing she'd done. He confessed to her about a few things from his not-so-clean past, including his previous gambling problem and how he had kicked it well before they met. It was true, at least in the way an addiction can ever be considered kicked.

He shouts upstairs, "I'm just going for a lie-down, love. Let me know if the water gets cold."

No reply, but that's standard when Judith bathes. She hates to ruin the experience with chatter and normally scolds him if he tries to talk to her before she's out of the bath. He lies down on the couch, eyes closed. But his mind is wide open, and the bad thoughts come. He pulls more hair out and realises there is zero chance he will be able to get any sleep, so he gets off the couch, does one push-up, and walks back to the kitchen to put the kettle back on.

Someone knocks at the door.

Tom runs back into the living room and ducks behind the couch, as though the knocker has X-ray vision.

"Tom!"

His breathing increases rapidly, he is very conscious of it, and he is sure whoever is at the door will hear it.

"Tom! It's Irene from the apartment next door. Are you okay?"

She knocks again, and Tom tries to squeeze into an even smaller shape. Irene shouts through the door, "Tom, I'm coming back with a key. I haven't seen you or Judith for a few days. I'm worried."

There is some relief that it's only Irene, but he doesn't want the nosy old bag coming back. He curses Judith for giving her a key and not getting it back. He estimates that it's been nearly a year since they went away and left it with her.

He straightens up and shouts from behind the couch "Irene, it's all good. I'm not decent, though, and Judith has gone to stay at her sister's for a while."

"Oh, okay. Did you take your garbage out, by the way?"

When he hears her footsteps moving away, he gets up, moves back in the kitchen and makes two teas with unwashed cups: one for his wife and one for himself. He takes them up to the bathroom and places them on the edge of the bath, next to the cup he made earlier.

"Have some tea, darling. You look cold. This will warm you up," he says.

He smiles at her before disrobing and stepping into the water, "Room for one more?"

As Tom squeezes in on the opposite side of Judith, being careful not to disturb her, there's a loud knock on the door—one with a sense of urgency.

"Tom, are you in there?" a male voice shouts.

He takes a gulp of tea and swills it around his mouth.

He'd considered calling it in as an accident when it happened. That's why he put a dead bulb in the landing area and moved the vacuum to the top of the stairs — tripping over it three times since. In a way, it was an accident. He tried to convince himself of that, anyway.

"I think we're going to need more scented candles," Tom says as he leans over and kisses his wife on the forehead.

The thought of living without her was too much to bear. Not to mention the additional lies and deceit that would be required.

She died for nothing.

Work is onto him now anyway, the emails from his boss and the voicemails urgently asking to see him. He feels like the deer from the nature documentary.

There's another loud knock at the door. "Tom!"

Tom stands up and reaches across to the cabinet to retrieve the small brown packet and then sits back down on the edge of the bathtub.

He didn't mean for her to fall down the stairs; he was only trying to stop her from calling the police. He had grabbed the arm of her nightgown and, when she yanked it away, she lost her balance and tumbled all the way down. She moaned for a while—an awful wail that has stayed with him over the last few days. He won't miss that.

"Tom!"

He just wanted to unload, share the burden, work through it before it got out of control. If they came up with a plan, they could probably find a way to put the money back before anyone noticed and then he could get help again. Going to prison wasn't an option. He wasn't cut out for that.

He should have known. Judith was always so black and white.

She is now.

"I love you, Judith," he says as he empties the packet into his cup before taking a large gulp of tea.

She's Dead

She's dead. Behind the eyes, I mean.

She moves the items over the barcode scanner with undeniable poetry, but it isn't rocket science. For a moment, I consider the idea of a checkout monkey and a little giggle sneaks out, but alas nothing from — what's her name? Bethany. That's the name on the badge anyway. What a funny name for a chimp that would be. And then I think, what wouldn't be? Monica? Marge?

The explosion sends me reeling to the floor in a thunderclap of shattered glass. I feel some of it pierce the right side of my body, but no pain registers. There is a ringing in my ears. Blood begins to seep through my crisp white shirt, and I wonder how I'll ever get it out.

I see someone slowly get up. A young man, perhaps in his twenties. He dusts himself off with his good hand. His other arm is on the floor next to a green basket. He glances around, and I follow his gaze across the debris. We catch sight of each other. I have never seen him before, yet I feel close to him.

My body starts to sting as the shock wears off and I push myself up. The conveyer belt is covered in broken glass. I'll need to put that lettuce back.

I turn to face Bethany. Her face is a mess, cut to shreds by shards of glass that remain embedded in her skin. They sparkle in the evening sun like diamonds.

I start to move towards her, and she looks directly at me for the first time. Something isn't right. Shock can affect people in different ways, but her eyes are as dead as they were before. No sign of trauma. She turns back to the conveyor belt, picks up the juice and puts it through, then roughly grabs the lettuce and asks if I want to change it for another.

The ringing in my ear starts to subside and I can hear the sounds of people screaming and crying for help.

Bethany has just asked if I want to change my lettuce.

I scream at her then, "What's wrong with you?"

"It has a caterpillar on it," she replies sheepishly.

"Are you insane, woman?" I scream at her again.

For the first time, I see some fear in her eyes. It gives me some satisfaction.

Someone is pulling at my shirt, "Hey, buddy, are you okay?"

I turn around and see the guy from earlier, but the closeness has gone. He is unscathed, unmarked, both arms intact.

The manager approaches the next checkout with a broom and starts sweeping the broken jar from the floor.

It's happened again.

I need help. I've been back three months now, but it isn't getting better.

I look towards the street outside and can see the enemy all around. The reflection in the window projects a much younger version of myself—gun in hand, full uniform—ready for action.

Thorns

It wasn't always like this. I was happy once.

I remember the bucket of blackberries went flying the day he shoved me into the bush by the side of the old railway track, the slow motion flurry of dark fruit scattering the ground like big juicy hailstones. Laughter followed, of course, prompted as though from a '70s TV show, only with the bully holding the cue cards and directing proceedings. The arching shoots entrapped me and prolonged the comedy as I tried to wrestle free, and the thorns of the plant lacerated my face and legs. As I placed my hand down on the ground to thrust myself upward, I felt one of the thorns pierce my skin and then break off inside. Finally, I broke free, tears streaming down my fruit-smeared face, and I wished him dead. My hand throbbed as I ran home to wish him dead some more and to nurse the wound but found nothing.

I woke up that night with the sensation that my hand was on fire. After switching the lamp on, I had tried to scream, but only rasps came out as I watched the blackness ink its way through the veins of my hand to my wrist and arm, rooting its way through me and establishing itself like the stubborn bush from the railway track.

And then it faded.

That day was the beginning of his vendetta, and I still have no idea why he singled me out. I asked him once, and he simply replied, "I don't know."

For someone without a clear motive, Billy is incredibly driven, as though his sole purpose in life is to destroy mine, and he is very adept with his disciples in tow. They torment me in class, but it doesn't end there. They wait outside the gates. They email me and text. They are everywhere. They are in my head. They exist.

Often I get home late as I wait on the school grounds for them to leave, and sometimes they do, but frequently they come and look for me. There are six of them now.

His influence is growing, and it's getting hard to find a place to hide. It's getting hard to hide the tears and the bruises, too.

Each encounter is getting progressively worse, and the hate inside me is growing stronger, as is the network of black roots that have spread and no longer fade. They are in my system now, and part of me, and I have to wear long sleeves that cover my hands and my mum's foundation to cover the ones that are creeping up my neck. The burning sensation accompanies the growth and feeds on the hate like a fire consuming oxygen, and sometimes I wake up thinking my entire body is aflame.

On more than one occasion I have contemplated ending my life, but there has usually been a place in my head I can travel to in search of solace, a colourful wonderland of hope and innocence where I can create my own adventures and rule the world.

Today I can't find it.

I can feel the roots coiling themselves around my brain as though taking ownership of an old derelict piece of real estate. I know it's been growing inside me since the day at the rail track and slowly possessing every part of me, but it is the first time I have felt them in my head. Like thorny climbers threading their rampant paths, they are shutting down my havens one at a time, and I am left blindly stumbling through a jungle of twisted vegetation as I try to find my wonderland.

I sense the evil and can feel the poison injected by the spiky spines that penetrate. The dark thoughts are closing in like thunderclouds preparing themselves for an apocalyptic finale, and I can't find my shelter. I have tried to starve them, but the bleakness and hopelessness of my life seem to be the only sustenance they need now.

The voices are new. They started an hour ago. "Get out there and bring some hell to their day," the last one whispered, the unmistakable sound of fire crackling in the background.

I know it's the Devil. Who else would it be?

I have tried fighting. God knows I have tried. But I don't have any fight left, and God isn't here with me now.

I give myself over, surrender, and feel the final flurries of growth without resistance.

There's a feeling of power and control surging through me and, for the first time in ages, I have my purpose now. I open the front door and walk outside into the street, and the lightning starts, as do the screams and the killing.

Not everyone is screaming. A contrasting indifference and resoluteness seem to be written across some of the other faces as they continue to their destinations, apathetic to the carnage and blood that surrounds them. Are these people carrying their own thorns and uprising in retaliation for all the evil committed against them?

I question now who is running the show. Is this a judgement day of sorts?

If that is the case, perhaps it isn't the Devil in charge after all.

There are many questions rushing through my head as I grip the knife tightly and make my way through the hysteria. My intention is unwavering, though, and I have never felt surer of anything in my life.

I have spent my whole life hiding. No more.

I'm coming for you, Billy.

Stick or Twist

Jesus Christ, I killed the cat! was the thought that stayed with me for some time after it happened.

She died on a Saturday. I remember as it was one of those beautiful sunny spring days in Australia with the smell of smoke in the air from nearby farms that were burning off. Now, every time that smoky haze seeps through town, the first thing that comes to mind is me standing on the patio staring at the bloody mess that had been crammed into our post box.

That was thirteen years ago, and as I sit and write this down for all to see, I want to be clear that I am not asking for forgiveness, but I want to get this off my chest.

My dad said it must have been an accident. His affection for cats was limited like mine, but I thought that might have been pushing it. It looked as though the cat had been turned inside out and then slam-dunked into a hole much smaller than you would ever imagine it could fit.

I suppose at the time he was trying to protect me.

I couldn't bring myself to say anything to my dad about the bet, and my mum was unapproachable, lost in her own world.

While going snooping for Christmas presents last year, I stumbled upon a bunch of letters from her lover, lots of them, and even a half-naked photograph with the name John on the back and an X beneath. That was something no child should ever have to see, and I always thought this was more macabre than the fiction I was reading at the time—but at least you could close a book.

I had no physical part in the cat's death and, even at that stage, as a naive eleven-year-old boy, I wasn't convinced it was my doing. It was just a silly game.

Let me explain.

I was a relatively lonely—and only—child and this often involved playing card games with make-believe people. If I won, something wonderful would happen, and if I lost there would be a pre-determined forfeit. For example, if I won, I would become a popular kid at school, and if I lost, I would puke at school during gym class. If I won, I would get an A for English, and if I lost, I would lose one of my shoes. These were all just examples of how silly and harmless the whole thing was supposed to be.

At this point, I should say that I loved English class at school, and it was my aspiration to become a writer. I suppose I was setting myself a challenge with only an ineffectual consequence if I failed. One thing for sure is I wanted it and would do almost anything to make sure it happened. There were a lot of sacrifices to make sure I got A's, too many to mention.

So back to that day. My dad had just gone to work with his flask in hand for the evening shift, and my mum was on her way to see lover boy with an inch-thick layer of make-up on her face and enough perfume to make me gag.

Yahtzee was the game today; indeed, I was running my very own mini Vegas—VIP only of course. My record was 402 at the time. If I beat that score, I would find a ten dollar note in the house so I could go and get some junk food from the milk bar, and if I lost, our cat would die. Jesus, I know!

So there you have it, ten dollars or a dead cat and of course now I look back on that with guilt and regret but also wryly think why only ten dollars.

I scored 402 on my fifth attempt, and that was no mean feat. I didn't officially beat the score, but surely that effort wouldn't go unappreciated.

I searched the house from top to bottom in the hope that this might still count as a win. All I found was fifty cents and my Dad's porn collection.

It was Friday morning and I was getting my books together for school when the ten-dollar note slid out of my English essay book. Brand new, shiny and eager to be spent, I pocketed the cash enthusiastically and planned a visit to the milk bar en route to school. Before I left that day, I looked in on the cat to make sure she was still alive. Sally was eating what would be her last meal, and only briefly tilted her head towards me; I gave her the finger and skipped to the milk bar feeling like a millionaire. On the way to the shop I considered how the ten-dollar note got into that book, and the only logical conclusion I could draw was that it was a treat from my parents for getting an A on my English essay the previous week.

When I got home that night, I thanked my mum for the money. She said she had no idea where it came from, and that my dad must have put it there. She said this with a whiff of resentment as she always assumed, and rightly so, that my dad and I had a much stronger relationship.

The next day, before I had the chance to ask my Dad about the money, we found the dead cat stuffed into the post box. Well, my mum found it and came screaming into the house, waking my dad up after a long night shift. I was told to wait in the house, but I was keen to see what was going on. I followed them out on to the porch and saw my dad standing there in his underpants, scratching his head. I remember thinking for a brief moment he was definitely more Columbo than Sherlock, and that was okay. Columbo was my favourite anyway.

The two years that followed passed without event, and the feeling of guilt slowly subsided. I also made a vow never to use another living being as a consequence of losing a silly game.

Until … B+ for English!

I was traumatised by that grade for a while; I couldn't let it happen again.

Take a day off my life for an A in my next English essay.

It was the first time I brought my own mortality into these twisted deals, and I hoped one day would be enough to secure the grade. It seemed to do the trick, and for the next two years, I never dropped below an A.

The affair was still continuing. I caught my mum on the phone one night talking to loverboy. She didn't know I was in earshot and whined on that this wasn't the life she wanted to lead, and I even heard her ask him when they were going to make a proper go of it. My dad was becoming even more of a shadow of himself and seemed resigned to his second-rate life. He never admitted it but looking back I think he knew about the affair.

Weeks passed, and I was gradually getting more withdrawn at school. The teachers were noticing, and there was even that question at parent-teacher night, "Is everything okay at home?"

No, not really, my mum is a bitch and a whore, and my dad is dead behind the eyes.

I recall my mum gave me a pep talk after the parent and teacher meet.

"You need to break out of your shell, Mark,' she said. "Nobody will ever take you seriously if you can't mix socially, will they, Jim?"

"No. No, love. No."

"You have to start making an effort. The way you behave reflects on us, Mark. You have to pick your game up."

I remember staring at the back of her head as she droned on in the passenger seat, and imagining it exploding into a million pieces. It would be a bit of a mess, but I would help my dad clean the car up and, after that, we could go and get lemonade and chips and watch Starsky and Hutch.

I was starting to make a bit more of an effort at school; my dexterity with a pack of cards certainly helped. A few card tricks and some fancy shuffling was all it took to get a little following. The last few years' practising was starting to pay off. The morning before school was my favourite time. I even started a pre-class Blackjack tournament in the common room. We paid someone to stand lookout; if they saw a teacher coming, they would cough, and we would throw our textbooks on the table.

I dominated.

Everything was starting to fall into place— until the school bully Richard tried his luck and lost his money on a stupid bet. He subsequently pinned me to the wall, punched me in the belly full force, and made me give him the money back.

The resentment within me was growing rapidly, and the thought of someone spoiling the very limited fun I had in life was unbearable. A thought popped into my head, and it was fleeting but sinister.

Take a day from my life but make him pay.

I had broken the vow to keep others out of this—an emotional reaction to an idiot. I couldn't control it, the thought just entered my head. I don't think thoughts can be filtered; they're instinctive. Christ, if every thought manifested into the physical form, there'd be a whole world of trouble.

I didn't think anything of it for the rest of the day. It was only on the way home after English class that I recalled the thought and regretted it immediately. Another essay had come back with an A+ and a wink from Mr. Dermott. Things were looking up, and I considered alternatives ways to sort out the Richard situation.

The next day he came to school unharmed. I was relieved. The cat's death was perhaps a coincidence after all. On the other hand, Richard was still being a prick, and even more so since the Blackjack incident. He started spreading rumours that I liked to look at boys' cocks in the showers, that I still suckled from my mum's breasts and that my dad was a paedophile. I don't think anyone truly believed these were true, but it didn't stop them getting on the bandwagon. The influence of the bully is powerful, and popularity is everything as a child.

The next night I made sure it was more than just a fleeting thought.

Three days from my life and make him pay.

Nothing.

We had eggs thrown at the house one night. I didn't see who threw them, but I made an educated guess. My mum's response was quite exceptional.

"Mark, are these your friends?"

Yes, this is what friends do. We throw eggs at each other's houses, and if we really like each other, we take a shit into our hands and rub it on the front door.

The feeling of rage and exclusion was starting to take its toll.

Five days from my life and make him pay!

The next day Richard turned up at school sporting a large gash in his leg. It needed six stitches, and he spent the day showing it off to all the girls, and they all wooed and gasped admiringly. At school, it seemed if you sported an injury from a BMX or a skateboard, suddenly you were God's gift. All I had succeeded in doing was boosting his popularity.

The kid was really starting to give me grief. He sat three rows behind me in English and did everything he could to disrupt the class. Various projectiles would be thrown my way, and he had free rein to be loud and obnoxious. Mrs. Curtis had no control. Enough was enough.

One month from my life and make him pay!

It was a car accident: a woman reversed out of her driveway and apparently did not see the BMX behind her. She was busy getting her two-year-old ready for pre-school and was already running late for work, and for that tardiness she now had a thirteen-year-old boy's death on her conscience for the rest of her life. That wasn't how it was supposed to happen, there wasn't supposed to be anyone else involved—it wasn't part of the deal—and he was only supposed to be badly injured, not killed.

The deal?

I later found out his mum committed suicide. The ripples of the event didn't occur to me immediately—I was thirteen, and the one person in my way was dead.

I understand that I'm not painting a very pleasant picture of myself, but, as I have stated, I am not looking for forgiveness. I just want to provide some form of explanation to all that were affected by my actions.

For a few days after the accident, the mood of the teachers and children at the school was very sombre, but it wasn't long before things returned to normal. It turns out most people thought Richard was an ass. I later found out that his dad was an alcoholic and used to beat him—a lot. I'm sure he must have had people in his life that loved and cared for him and for those people, I am genuinely heartbroken and remorseful.

Life carried on without event for a few months, and I was even moderately happy. It seemed to be getting easier to put things behind me. I was still getting A's for English and, of course, still offering days of my life to increase the odds in my favour.

I still tried to put Richard's death down to a coincidence—there was no possible way I could have influenced such a chain of events. I played the game but only as a way of dealing with things and to make my life seem more bearable, more exciting.

You're just a slag!

My mum was in the kitchen working through a stack of ironing that looked like the leaning tower of Pisa: gravity-defeating pants and towels that would be methodically steamed as though she was cleansing her soul for her actions.

"Mark, where's your other trainer?" she screamed suddenly.

"I don't know. Is it not in my school bag?" I replied with my familiar nervous tone.

To this day, I don't know what triggered her over-reaction. Maybe the promises from loverboy were not so genuine. She stomped down the hallway, threw my door wide open, put the bag on my head and screamed, "Does it look like it's fucking in there?"

I cried, and I don't mind admitting that. I sat blubbing for a good few minutes after she had marched angrily back to the kitchen to continue ironing the crap out of a dishcloth. I thought I had uttered the words under my breath, an angry, but very quiet protest.

"You're just a slag!"

I felt the door swing open again and then the sting of her hand on my cheek, which I could still feel a good few minutes later.

"Wait until your Dad gets in!"

A year of my life for loverboy to die!

For a few hours, I locked myself in my bedroom. I remember thinking *what is my move here?*

I heard my dad's car pull up, and the door open, the sound of my mum's dulcet and fake sorrowful tones greeting him at the door. My dad came barging into my room then. Usually, he knocked, but not that day. He asked me to go into the living room and to pull my pants down and bend over. The look on his face was vacant, like something from the body snatchers movie.

There was only one strike with the belt, but it was a beauty. I thought my dad might have gone easy on me, but everyone has a dark side, and he let rip, perhaps with all the pent-up frustration that life had not turned out as planned. Afterwards, I could see the event had drained him. He looked beaten, and his eyes had already moistened with regret. My mum, however, seemed relatively satisfied, especially after the forced apology.

"Sorry for calling you a slag, Mum," I said.

"That is not a nice word, Mark. You shouldn't use words that you don't understand the meaning of."

Slag!

John fell off a ladder and was almost split in two, apparently. It was a Sunday morning, and he was touching up the exterior paint on the roof edge. There was a huge gust of wind on what was otherwise a very calm day, and he fell and impaled himself on the neighbours' wrought iron fence. I found all of this out when I overheard my mum confessing everything to my dad.

It was getting more and more difficult for me to pass these events off as coincidence. I knew I had potentially played a part in the demise of three living beings.

For days my mum sat staring solemnly into space. Home life had become even more unbearable. My dad kept his cowardly distance, and Mum was reduced to a few grunts here and there. Mealtimes were awful, and I couldn't wait to rip myself away.

My English papers kept coming back with A's, and I became even more obsessed with writing stories. It was my escape and a chance to place myself in any situation I chose.

I would write all weekend, sometimes until after midnight. I was adamant this would be my ticket out of a humdrum existence.

At sixteen, I had my first short story published in the local rag. It took fifteen attempts and the final stake or offer or whatever sordid name you want to give it was six months. Life continued like that for a while. I had a small group of friends, and we would get together infrequently for card games or to mess around with computers. I still felt very detached, but that was fine; I was on my way to becoming the next Stephen King, and everything was falling into place.

The night before I went to university, my parents finally split up. Now, in hindsight, this might have been a better alternative as the house jackpot: a simple split without casualties. If I had not let anger rule my thoughts back then, it certainly would have been a consideration. I wanted to hurt my mum, though, as she had hurt me and it's difficult to channel that anger and rationalise at such a young age.

University was great; finally, I was around like-minded individuals who enjoyed writing and talking about their stories and processes. I felt as though I belonged somewhere, and life was beginning to fall into place.

I graduated with a first class honours in English, and a few published short stories in local magazines. The stage was set, and some of my pieces were getting attention from local publishers. I was asked to submit a short story for consideration for an anthology of fiction.

Please let this happen — three years from my life.

I didn't want to undercut this. I still had no idea how this worked, but I know from experience if the offer was low, there was a chance it would not happen. It took a while to go through the publishing process, but after a few edits, phone calls, sleepless nights, and a hell of a lot of waiting, the book was finally published three days before I turned twenty-three. It was a massive day. I invited my parents around to celebrate. They had both remarried and seemed to be happier. Life seemed to be ebbing back into both. I was so proud of this achievement and even convinced myself that it was my genuine talent that had led to this.

The anthology was successful, and my name was as plain as day in the credits for all to see. I was a published author.

The book sold well, and I was subsequently contacted by a larger publishing house, one that's well known worldwide. They wanted to commission a short story. No guidelines were provided, just a short fiction or non-fiction piece.

Three years for this one to be successful would be the last deal I would make—that was a promise to myself.

***

Since starting this story, I have been getting some sharp pains down the left side of my body, and I have a sense that someone or something is here with me. I have had that feeling before. The cost of this success has come at a high price, and now I sit here contemplating how many chips I've thrown into the pot and how much I've lost over the years. As a child, the days were long and time seemed infinite.

From the corner of my eye, I can now see it, a smudge of darkness impatiently sweeping from one side of the room to the other. I think it's waiting for me to finish my final piece.

Each time I played those games of cards with made-up people, I felt something: a presence, a feeling that I wasn't as alone as I thought I was. Each time I made an offer, I felt too far removed to feel totally responsible. But I knew better than that. And now I can see it and can only assume it has come for me.

It has been with me from an early age. And it's impossible to win against a stacked house.

It feels as though the air in the room is getting heavy and there is darkness surrounding my vision now, and ever so slightly it is creeping in; my breath is no longer consistent but chaotic and uneasy.

The game got easier with time, too easy, and I've hurt a lot of people. My death at twenty-four will also hurt my parents and potentially others. I am sorry for all the pain that I have caused.

I am all in now, and I doubt this is the kind of house where one can get credit.

The only consolation I have … *there it is again, and I can feel the blackness filling my soul now. I'm scared* … is that this will be my best piece yet. How successful it will be is hard to say, and whether or not it's down to real talent I'll never know, but at least it will be publishe

Child

There is an evil about him that goes beyond the worst I have read in books or seen in movies, an evil far more threatening than the shadowy figures I bring to life in my stories. The moments when I catch his eye make my skin prickle and my body shudder. It feels like he's running his fingers up and down my spine, and the coldness lingers deep inside me for hours afterward.

My fascination with dark fiction exposes me to all sorts of menace, but nothing ever comes close to the man that only I can see. I was ten when the visions first started and, as I got older, they gradually became more frequent. I am thirteen now and, until the last week, I'd been seeing him almost every day. In the beginning, he appeared as a blurry shadow out of the corner of my eye, but each day his presence has become more defined and lingers a little bit longer. I've seen him outside of the house, too: at school, the supermarket, the park—everywhere. The same taunting smile greets me every time, and he's always wearing the long dark leather trench coat that completes his ominous manifestation.

Upon first glance, there is a handsomeness to him: pitch black hair, matching stubble, sharp features, and a strong chin with crystal blue eyes that suggest purity. When he fixes me in his cold gaze and smiles, an innate ugliness consumes him. His eyes turn black, and any humanity fades. It is more than a look of disdain, as though it is causing him pain not to reach inside my chest and rip my heart out. His smell is overpowering—rotting meat doused with cheap aftershave—and lingers for hours after he visits.

I live in fear.

At bedtime, I don't let myself relax, afraid that he might materialise from the darkness. My body lies rigid, eyes fixed on the corner of the room where the moonlight doesn't reach, and I lay there praying for him not to appear. Eventually I fall asleep, but sometimes he steps out from behind the closet, and I run screaming into my mum's room, the sound of his taunting laughter not far behind.

My mum says it's just a phase, like having an invisible friend, but she's looked more than a little concerned of late. The interrupted nights and worry for me have depleted her to the point of exhaustion, and I feel guilty for that.

In a desperate attempt, she took me to see a psychiatrist a few weeks ago, a middle-aged lady called Doctor Roper. But, as expected, The Man appeared in the session and at one point stood behind the doctor with his hands around her neck, mimicking strangulation. I was too scared to speak.

"Tom, take a lollipop and go and sit in reception for a few minutes, please," Dr. Roper said.

Five minutes later, my mum came out with smudged mascara and tears down her cheeks.

I love her. I know she must have been through so much after dad died, but that was so long ago now. Although it still feels like a dark cloud hovers over our lives. There have been a couple of men in her life over the years—Brian was the coolest, and I hoped he might become part of our family, someone I could perhaps call Dad. Towards the end of their relationship, she started treating him badly and kept pushing him away, and, eventually, he never came back.

Mum pretends to be strong, but I know it's just an act. Sometimes I hear her crying in her room. I want to comfort her, but I don't know what to say. If she's having a particularly bad week, I bring her breakfast in bed. She doesn't even care when I burn the bacon.

I want to see her smile more often. It makes me feel warm inside when she does. But all I seem to do is worry her.

I frequently wonder what happened to my dad. How he died. I didn't know him, and Mum hasn't told me much. If I even mention him, she shuts down. It doesn't seem fair, but I don't want to cause any more distress than I already have.

My episodes with The Man have put extra pressure on us. I try not to bother her with it, but his presence has felt more malignant of late, and that terrifies me. Last week when I was sat at the kitchen table with my mum, he bent over and whispered in my ear that he was going to kill her and take her head back to hell as a trophy.

It's hard to tell what's real and what isn't anymore.

Days have passed since that threat with no sign of him. I try to convince myself that it was just a silly phase after all, a figment of my over-active imagination. Either way, the house is different without his presence, and things seem to be returning to normal. Last night I slept through for the first time in ages. Mum looks a lot less tired, too.

Now, as I lay in bed, I'm thinking about new characters for my next story. I even contemplate writing one about the man who's been tormenting me—perhaps as a form of closure. But that might be a bad idea, especially after the last few times. I get so engrossed in my stories it feels as though the monsters might suddenly jump off the page. Sometimes I can smell them and, if I really concentrate, I can hear their low guttural growls as if they are with me. During my last story, I even thought that I heard footsteps approaching from behind, and I got so scared I had to throw the pen down. I wonder if it's all just in my head, but that day I swore I felt hot air on the back of my neck. That's how I know I'm getting better at it.

As I am about to close my eyes, a scream rattles through the house. It's unlike any of the movie screams I've heard before; this one is more of a howl, raw and pained—blood-curdling.

I jump out of bed and rush down the hallway into my mum's room. The Man turns to look at me as I enter. He's straddling her on the bed with his hands wrapped around her neck, and he smiles his signature smile, unveiling the perfect white teeth that only serve to emphasise the darkness of his eyes. He begins to howl with obvious pleasure, removing one hand temporarily to beat his chest in celebration.

I feel as though I might pass out, and I lose all feeling in my legs. Frozen in place, all I can do is listen to my mum's croaks as he continues to choke her, her hands flailing in front of his face. She's turning an alarming shade of blue.

Eventually, the room stops spinning, and the dream-like sequence becomes all too real.

"It's been a long time coming, child," The Man screams.

I feel the warmth spread across the front of my pants, and I know he sees it, too.

"You're next, piss stick."

The mocking laughter that follows flicks a switch inside and my anger erupts.

I close my eyes and, with the darkness serving as a suitable blank canvas, my imagination beings to paint the worst. The fear has left now. My body trembles with hatred instead, and it fuels my creativity. Soon the spine-chilling cries begin as the first few creatures take form in the temporary dungeon I have created. They are frenzied and starved, and there are sounds of tearing flesh as they begin to feed on each other. Bloody saliva pours from mouths filled with razor-sharp teeth.

As I begin to unlock their makeshift cages, the monsters roar and scream with anticipation, yet they still feel two-dimensional—fine for my stories, but not good enough to save my mum. I will only have one shot at this. I need this creature to live, breathe, and feel; it must be authentic enough to be brought to life in this room. It needs desire, to be ravenous for murder and the accolade of most evil.

With my eyes still closed, I refocus. This is my last chance. I need to save her.

And then I am there, back in the darkness, but this is a new place, one I haven't been before. There is a putrid smell of death here so strong it makes me want to gag. In the middle of the drab concrete floor, a dark green pool of viscous liquid angrily fizzes and bubbles away. And then the first green vine slowly breaks the surface and begins to dance erratically, as though feeling out its surroundings.

It feels much more real this time. I am its creator, and I have given it life and purpose.

"I demand your presence here with me," I scream.

Before long, I hear raspy breathing in front of me, and the pungent smell of rotting vegetation fills my nostrils. The creature is born.

I hear a weak groan from the bed. *Mum.* I almost lose focus but keep my eyes shut tight and add the finishing touches to my creation.

Its green scaly exterior is fortified by hundreds of tendrils that are capable of latching onto their prey and holding them until there is no longer a need. The head is dark green and crowned with two large horn-shaped rocks. Its eyes are as black as coal and sit slightly above its oversized snout, its nostrils searching the air for its first meal.

The elongated mouth opens to reveal layers of razor-sharp teeth, and its tongue drips with a green substance that hisses as it lands on the wooden floor below.

I open my eyes and watch The Man release his grip around my mum's neck. He commands the creature to leave, announcing he is already doing the dark work. For a moment, I doubt myself and feel my legs start to go once again. The creature starts to fade, and The Man laughs and places his hands back around her neck. I briefly think that it might be too late.

"This is your fault, child."

I stare at the scene with mouth wide open. My concentration has gone and with it, my creature.

"She killed me, child. Put a knife straight through my chest," he says as he opens his trench coat, exposing the two-inch wound.

"She killed your daddy. But I'm back now, and I'm going to take care of you both."

I close my eyes again, and my mind explodes with confusion and rage. Soon the creature is back, but even more desperate and hungry. The roar is fiercer and more intentional this time. Its only sustenance so far has been the evil that I fed it, but it is present now in our world with all the smells and temptations of fresh human flesh. The creature quivers as though it is all too much, and the tendrils start to dance in the air like kite strings. Finally, they start to work together and slowly pierce through the air towards The Man. He releases his grip, and there is another plea for the creature to back down, but it doesn't help him this time. The creature has fully crossed over.

The tendrils hover a few inches from his face, and although he manages to knock a few away, they keep on coming. The first few launch their attack, coiling around his neck like serpents, and the scream that follows is satisfyingly human. Slowly they slither upwards, leaving a sticky trail on his skin. Then the first one enters his open mouth, and I see it snake its way down his throat. Others follow, and soon The Man is clawing at his neck and gasping for breath. The ones not already in his mouth twist and writhe around his body in excitement. Soon he is cocooned and incapable of movement.

As I finally open my eyes, not wanting to miss the moment, I see the tendrils hoist The Man's heart from his mouth. The lifeless body falls to the bed and, once again, the eyes fix on me. There isn't a smile this time, though, just a lifeless pose and an unnaturally swollen neck.

The creature roars once more and begins to feast on the heart.

I look towards the blood-painted face of my mum and can see she's starting to take in strained mouthfuls of air, unable to do anything but watch as my creation continues to dine on its prize. In only a few moments, The Man is stripped of most of his flesh, and his intestines lie glistening on the bed next to him. Once done, the creature begins to sniff the air again, ready for its next meal.

"Mum!"

The creature turns to look at me and bares its flesh-covered teeth as it sends its tendrils towards me. I close my eyes again and vision the beast back to the place it came from, but it is strong and is not going without a fight. I feel one of the tendrils slide against my cheek, and then dampness around my neck as others begin to slither their way around me. The pressure around my throat increases and, as I begin to struggle for air, I hear the creature move in towards me. It doesn't want to be locked away again; it has a taste for flesh now. All at once, I unleash the other monsters from their cages, but this time they feel even more real, as though I have taken them to the next level—this is getting easier.

The green tendrils work astonishingly fast, pinning them against the wall and ripping them to shreds one by one. There are limbs and heads flying everywhere, accompanied by an orchestra of vicious snarls and pained whimpers. But then I bring a strategy to the savagery, and I begin to flank it from the left with my earlier creations and, while it is busy making light work of them, my latest and worst rush in from the right. After a monumental struggle, they eventually manage to bring it down and drag it into its newly formed iron cage. The heavy gate falls behind it.

Finally, I open my eyes. Evil has left the room.

I run to my mum. She is in pain, but at least she is breathing. Her voice is hoarse and there are red marks around her neck, but we hold each other tight in the knowledge we are lucky to be alive.

As she begins to recover, she tells me she's been seeing him, too. Doctor Roper told her it was the guilt resurfacing, her brain playing tricks and projecting a physical manifestation of her inner turmoil.

"It wasn't guilt," she said. "I would do the same thing over again. Black and blue he used to beat me. But that wasn't the worst of it."

She goes on to explain that if she tried to resist, he'd threatened to hurt *the child*. That is what he used to call me apparently, *the child*. Not son.

"Something snapped inside him when he found out he was going to be a father. I refused to get an abortion, and that's when it all started. He didn't want to share me and punished me for loving you so much. We weren't even allowed to leave the house. He said he would kill us both if I ever tried. And then one afternoon I walked into your bedroom and found him holding a pillow over your head. That same night, I killed him. Took the largest knife I could find in the drawer and plunged it into his chest. And I am not sorry for that. He was an evil, manipulative bastard."

I guess he even bargained with the devil for a chance at vengeance.

The bruises and cuts plastered all over her body were enough to convince authorities that it was self-defence.

At last, I have my answers.

I understand now what made him so terrifying. This character was not a fabrication in a story; he was real—once human but with a soul tarnished by evil. His hate had continued to build even after death and was strong enough to bring him back into our lives.

I hope we have seen the last of him, but if he does return, I'll be ready for him.

Evil lurks in the tunnels of my mind, too.

Journey's End

The road snakes up into the hills just as I remember, and giant trees line either side for as far as I can see. Rumbling wind accompanies me, yet I do not feel its touch as adrenaline courses through my body. The trees are dancing wildly, and the clouds are rolling towards me, bringing their shroud of darkness—just like in the dream.

I left the car days ago and have been walking this route ever since, following the visions that invaded my sleep. Suburbia turned to country road a while back, and I am here now in the middle of God knows where, holding onto a thread of hope that this journey will offer clues to my son's whereabouts—and that he is still alive.

As I continue marching forward, my skin begins to prickle with trepidation. But I am committed to this journey, and besides, there is nothing for me back there. The remaining light quickly begins to fade under cloud cover and, in a matter of minutes, the day has been stolen. A heightened sense of foreboding grips me and, as if on cue, there is a sound of snapping twigs to the right. I quickly turn to see two fiery red eyes emerge from the darkness, and a huge growl explodes that forces me to the ground in child-like terror. My heart is pounding far too fast, and I am struggling to get any breath in as I cling hopelessly to the ground.

Suddenly more red eyes emerge at once from the cover of trees, too many to count, This wasn't in the dream. I hold my breath in fear that the owner of one of those pairs of eyes will soon launch after me, and I am suddenly sure this is how my life will end. Their breathing is deep and impossibly in unison, and I conjure up all sorts of demonic images that could be making such a sound. These red eyes are the only source of light now; they hang in the air like static embers.

I close my eyes tightly in anticipation of death and hope that it will be quick. The breathing stops and more wood crackles underfoot. This is it. Its snout must only be inches from my face as I hear the creature slowly inhale. My body stiffens with the expectation of pain, but suddenly, more roars and battle cries break out from in the distance, and there is a subsequent low guttural rumble of disappointment as I hear it turn and saunter back towards the trees.

When I open my eyes, I see an abundance of red orbs dancing frantically in the blackness and the sound of snarls and ripping flesh. I push myself to my feet and consider running, but almost immediately the fight is over and there is a series of fading whimpers as the loser assumedly staggers away in shame. Perhaps they were fighting over me, the pecking order of who gets to dine on my flesh first.

One of them steps out from the darkness to show itself; perhaps the victor basking in its glory. It ambles towards me and comes to rest only four feet away. I freeze, heart pumping intensely and my legs suddenly struggle to keep me upright. It resembles a German Shepherd, but not the domestic kind. Its red eyes sit atop an elongated snout that houses razor-sharp teeth still tarnished with its cannibalised victim. Its claws look unnaturally sharp, and patches of surrounding hair, where it has any, are matted in fresh blood. We are locked in a standoff and I am at its mercy. It takes another step forward and is now close enough to touch. Suddenly, it stamps its front right paw down, turns, and menacingly saunters off behind the trees once again. The other eyes disappear all at once, and again I am alone and left shaking in fear. When I am sure there's enough distance between us, I begin walking again.

I have been walking for so long—three days I have counted so far— without food and water, but I am bristling with adrenaline and crave nothing but answers.

More hours pass as I continue moving forward, head down, with a necessary conviction that this road will eventually provide some form of closure. But it seems to be going nowhere. I am beginning to think I am losing my mind, that I might have snapped.

"Caw!"

The harsh cry from behind pierces the air with impossible volume. Instinctively, I bring my hands to my ears, but only seem to trap the sound as it echoes around my mind. My brain feels as though it might explode, and I double over and retch, but the only thing that emerges is the caw that was reverberating inside my head.

I turn to look for the source: crows line every tree for as far as darkness will allow me to see. They occupy almost every branch, heads cocked and observing me with irrational interest. But nothing about why I am here or what is happening could be defined as ordinary.

The crows begin to shift restlessly from side to side as much as the crowded branches will accommodate, and suddenly the now-familiar feeling of fear grips me again as another shudder rattles down my spine. I turn slowly and begin to sprint down the road.

For a moment, all I can hear is the sound of blood pumping in my ears and my feet stomping on the ground beneath me, but then the cacophony of shrills and flapping wings ensues from behind. My feet continue to pound intensely, yet I can hear them quickly closing the gap. Glancing over my shoulder, I see the sinister black mass approaching, flapping and gliding effortlessly. They are now only a few feet away.

My fists clench tightly, and I face forward and run as fast as my legs can carry me. The road is rushing beneath me at a dizzying pace, and I'm feeling lightheaded as I try to get some oxygen in my lungs. When I lift my head, I spot the wooden hut in the distance—and the noise behind ceases immediately. I turn my head again and there is nothing now but the road and empty trees. I grind to a clumsy halt.

The cabin is about a hundred feet in the distance, and this is far as the dream took me—the last stop. After the dream, I only remember feeling an obligatory need to follow the path it had showed me.

Three weeks have passed since Oscar was taken from us, and I've been floating in the abyss ever since. This journey has been a welcome distraction, but I suspect it might be more than that.

I continue onwards, nervously glancing around. There is some relief when I finally reach the cabin and the perceived safety of four walls.

The hefty door swings inward with a push—helped by the accelerating wind. I close the door behind me and momentarily zone out, trying to understand why I have been brought to this ten-foot square hut.

Looking out from each of the windows, I can see only the faint outline of sturdy oaks in the darkness. On the back wall of the cabin is a stove that I assume is gas powered. Two dirty saucepans rest on it. Next to it is a small cupboard with two drawers, no doubt housing some cutlery and cooking equipment. I pull a chair out from the table and sit as I feel some protection from the madness outside.

It was the longest night of our lives when he didn't come home. Rachel immediately assumed the worst, but I wouldn't let myself entertain anything other than a mischievous stunt. She phoned the police while I went out with my torch checking every inch of the garden, yelling that he wouldn't be in trouble if he came out. Then I checked the neighbour's gardens, and then the park, and repeated the process until well after midnight.

Rachel and I are still trying to find a way through the fog, but we keep dragging each other back to its centre. I know she blames me, holds me responsible—she said so. A week after his disappearance, she looked me in the eyes and said with sincere conviction, "Tom, I will never be able to look at you without blame." Her eyes were red and tears rolled down her cheeks.

We relied on Oscar relentlessly to lift our days. But I couldn't find him, and neither could the police. The knot in my stomach feels as though it is growing daily, applying ever increasing pressure in my chest, a relentless reminder of my guilt. I hate myself for saying it, but some small part of me wants to get on with the grieving. This limbo is unbearable.

I push myself up from the chair and switch on the stove. It lights on the first attempt, and momentarily I am back in our family kitchen in better times with the sounds of Oscar's laughter in the background. I turn it off and open the adjacent drawer: empty apart from a few forks and knives. But as I close it, something catches my eye on the floor jutting out from under the cupboard. I crouch down and pick up the Batman Lego figure. As I twirl it between my fingers, my hand is visibly shaking, and there is an immediate and uncomfortable tightness across my chest. I recall the excitement in his face as he ripped open the packet, such an enormous amount of joy for something so small and inexpensive.

I am certain it is his. My son was here, in this cabin. I am sure of it. I know it's why I have been led here.

I remember the day so vividly. Oscar was swinging from the makeshift swing that hung from the large bough of the old oak tree. He much preferred it to the plastic playset in the park. The wind was howling and the children on the roundabout were taking advantage of the extra help, screaming and laughing with fear and joy. I recall the abundance of crows in the trees, and how vocal they were. Perhaps they were trying to warn me, let me know that evil was present. A middle-aged woman was struggling to pull a German Shepherd as it stubbornly watched and frantically barked along in excitement. Or perhaps it was also trying to warn me.

It was only for two minutes. A stupid phone call from work that I will forever wish I had let go to voicemail. It was impossible to hear anything over the noise of the screaming kids, but I couldn't have walked more than forty feet away. When I returned, he was nowhere to be seen.

I have never experienced such a level of panic before. It was as if my brain malfunctioned and was unable to process the details. I remember rushing up to the other parents and screaming at them, demanding to know where he went. But not one person saw. It was as if he was never there. One of the little boys Oscar had been playing with said he saw him run towards the trees, but he couldn't remember which direction because he was on the roundabout at the time. I shook him far too roughly by the shoulders and begged him to remember.

But he couldn't.

I wipe away the moisture that is forming in my eyes. It's not the time for that yet. I'm on the right track, and it's time to move on. I must finish this journey.

There is a single sharp shrill from outside, and I exit the cabin to find the crows are back. They fill the trees ahead of me.

I grip the Lego figure tightly in my hand and continue down the road.

As I glance into the tree line, I note that the birds are less agitated this time and seem content merely as spectators. The wind continues to get audibly louder, squalling around me and savagely pummelling the tall trees that bend and creak in its path. The red eyes behind the trees are also back, but line both sides of the road this time. They seem to be tracking me, yet this time I feel no threat from them.

Another chunk of time is swallowed by this seemingly endless road, and the blanket of cloud makes it impossible to tell what time of day it is anymore. I am growing sick of darkness now, hungry to find some peace and to see the light again.

There is another loud caw, and I immediately look toward it. Nestled back from the road, almost invisible above the overgrown bushes where the crow is perched, I make out the outline of a chimney. I could easily have missed it. There are no streetlights and the house is unlit. The other crows start to move restlessly on their branches once again, and the breathing behind the tree line becomes faster and heavier.

After carefully creeping through a gap in the foliage, I rest my forehead against the dirty window of the rundown shack but cannot see anything through the grime. Working my way around, I try the front door, but, of course, it is locked. I edge around to the side of the house and find a window that is slightly ajar. It allows me to squeeze my hand through, and I gently prise it open, giving myself enough space to climb in. Heaving myself over, I carefully extend my hands towards the wooden floor and let myself down as gently as possible. It smells just as I imagined: damp and dirty—neglected.

There is too little furniture for the size of the room. The two couches facing each other are old, and the bottom trim is black with filth. There is an old melamine coffee table with exposed corners and a single coaster stained with faded browns. The rug beneath is threadbare and only the faintest outline of a pattern is visible.

There is nothing to suggest this house sees any love.

A pizza box sits atop the sideboard next to an empty bottle of liquor. The sole piece of art in the room is above the fireplace on the front wall: a huge blown-up picture of a deer, its hindquarters illuminated by rays of sunlight that make their way down through the canvas of trees. Beneath it, some burnt coal sits behind its rusty cage.

I'm not sure what I was expecting, but I suddenly feel out of place and begin to contemplate what the hell I'm doing. Perhaps the owner has a gun. I am trespassing, and this could end quickly—without answers. It's the first house I've come across, and I have nothing concrete to warrant being here, just a hunch provided by a dream and plastic toy. What do I do now?

I'm drawn to the stack of newspapers on the coffee table, but as I near its edge, the floor creaks far too loudly. I pause, expecting to hear a voice and footsteps. But silence prevails, aside from the relentless wind that whistles outside.

As I rifle through the newspapers one by one, I find jagged lines where pages have been ripped out. My body begins to tingle with adrenaline. Perhaps I am on the right track after all. On the bottom shelf of the table, there is a comic and a small sketch pad. Both look new. Opening the pad in the middle, I find only blank pages. But when I flick to the beginning, I momentarily feel as though the floor has fallen out from beneath me.

The drawing of Batman with oversized ears is one I have witnessed Oscar draw countless times. There is a smudge on the side of his cape, and I picture a tear falling from my son's face, one induced by confusion and fear. I can only imagine how terrified he must have been.

I pick up the coffee table and hurl it across the other side of the room. As it smashes against the wall, one of the legs breaks off, and a large crack appears down its centre when it falls back to the floor with a dull thud.

My body is trembling violently.

This person took my son from me. From us.

I realise I have given up my advantage and scramble behind the couch as I hear a thump from upstairs and the creak of floorboards above me. The feet are coming down the stairs now, and I peek from behind the couch to see the silhouette of a small-framed man emerge. He has only a few hairs sprouting from his head, and as he steps down from the final stair, I know I am looking at the man who took my son. I know.

The unarmed man surveys the room and, with laboured breathing, drags the coffee table away from the wall and begins to pick up the scattered paraphernalia. He takes another look around before walking to the window and closing it. Part of me wants to launch now, to rip him to shreds, but I hold back. I'm not sure why.

As he works his way around the room, I hold my breath and make myself as small as possible. His feet stop only inches from my face before moving slowly to the mantelpiece and grabbing the picture of the deer with both hands. I am confused by what he is doing, but when he removes the frame, it reveals a mass of newspaper clippings on the wall. I see him take something from the bottom part of the frame — it's a key — and then walks to the centre of the room sending the same loud creak echoing through the house.

He pauses for a moment and takes another look around before grabbing the end of the rug where the coffee table once stood. With a loud grunt, he yanks it away. As he crouches, his left hand reaches out for something, and then he begins to fumble with the key. Eventually, there is a click and, with one big wheeze, he lifts the trapdoor open. Its hinges squeak noisily, and all I can think about is Oscar being led down into the darkness. The man takes another look around before sticking his head into the hidden room.

There is a loud caw from outside that surprises us both. He momentarily lifts his head towards the front window and then stands up and guides himself down the steps.

I push myself up and move quickly towards the clippings.

Oscar.

I remember the picture we sent in, an old school photo of him with ruffled hair and toothy smile. The black and white clipping does not do him justice or capture the sparkle in his eyes. I run my finger across his lips, but it stops halfway as the adjacent story catches my eye.

Tom Grover, father of the missing child, Oscar Grover, found dead in a burnt-out car.

I stop myself from collapsing by reaching out to the nearby wall, and I begin to retch dry air. The room starts to fade into one large smudge of darkness, and I feel as though I am slipping away. There is a ringing in my ears, and my face begins to tingle. I am going to pass out. This would have all been for nothing. I focus on my breathing and try and slow it down. It cannot end now. Slowly, the feeling begins to pass, but I am left feeling lonelier than ever before and with an intense separation from the real world. I rip the article from the wall and note the date as three days ago. In darkness, and with the clipping shaking violently in hand, I read the first few lines of the story.

No. This cannot be happening. I am alive. I am here now.

"I am alive," I scream.

I read on. I can hardly believe my eyes as the reporter conjectures foul play, suicide for the murder of my child.

For the murder of my child.

"No. No. No."

This reporter knows nothing, feels nothing. Why would I hurt my child? He was everything to me.

My body is alive with fury, and every nerve ending is prickling with unease as I continue to scan the rest of the article. Car found two miles from city centre ... high blood alcohol level ... leaves behind his wife Rachel ... no other suspects at this time.

There is a picture of another child on the wall, too. This clipping is yellowing and much older. I note the date as nearly two years ago. The adjacent picture of who I assume to be his parents mentions a reward for information. All the articles are related to the disappearance of the Oscar and this other missing boy.

I can recall getting in the car and driving. I needed to be away from the house and all the reminders of my beautiful son. It was stifling. I couldn't breathe. I stopped off for a bottle of whisky and a packet of cigarettes—my first pack in twenty years. Before I took the first mouthful of liquor, I remember turning the stereo on full volume to block out the bad thoughts that kept swimming around. I remember drinking over half the bottle and spilling some as I lit the cigarette. There was a fleeting thought then that I could take all the grief away. After that, it becomes blank, a blur, a missing piece of history. And then I was walking, on an irrational whim, and following this path that I thought I had dreamt. But dead people don't dream.

Stooped over the hole in the floor, I take the first step down. The smell hits me immediately, and a cocktail of damp and mould fills my nostrils. There is a small light coming from a source somewhere at the back of the room.

And then his face comes into view, and he is staring directly at me.

I don't know what I feel at this moment—he looks so frail—but I remind myself that this is the person who turned my life upside down. His forehead is layered with deep wrinkles, and his skin looks coarse and sun beaten. The T-shirt he is wearing is far too large and hangs loosely from his tiny shoulders, but still exposes the excess belt strap that hangs unnaturally low.

I am struggling to understand why someone like this would do such a thing. What are the secrets behind those lines?

"Is he ... is he dead?" is all I can muster.

"I'm sorry," he wheezes.

And there it is, the closure I have been chasing.

"I knew you were coming," he says. "I saw it in my dream."

We stand and cautiously observe each other in this small world underneath his floor.

Behind him, I see an old mattress and a glass.

There was a small part of me that believed he might still be alive. But all hope has gone. I am empty.

"Why?" I ask. As if there could ever be a reason.

"I ... I am driven ... by a hunger," he replies, eyeing me as though I'm supposed to understand. "The same hunger that brought you back from the dead looking for an answer. It is part of you, your make-up. This is mine. I've been fighting it my whole life."

There's a small lamp on a desk that provides some dirty light against the back wall. I see a piece of clothing on the floor next to the mattress.

I cautiously move towards it while keeping an eye on my son's killer and bend over and retrieve the sweater. It is an Avengers one—his favourite—the one we used to struggle to get off him.

"I wanted to be caught," he says.

I lift the sweater to my nostrils, and I can smell him—his innocence, his fear, his love—and I begin to cry.

The man looks lost, almost sorry, but I know deep down something is broken. And he will continue until stopped.

There's a pleading in his eyes, and it's almost human. Almost. I bring fingers to my mouth and wolf-whistle. I didn't even know I could. Seconds afterward, there are multiple explosions of glass above and a raucous frenzy of growls and snarls. The animals pound the floor and shower sprinklings of dust around us. The man looks up nervously as one of them begins to sniff at the hole in the floor. And then the first one begins to navigate the stairs.

I look across at the old man. "Call them off, please. I'll turn myself in, I promise," he pleads.

There's a patch of wetness spreading across the front of his unwashed pants. And I am glad that he finally feels something more than his so-called hunger for murder.

I hold a finger up, and the beast stops reluctantly and lets out a single growl. It holds its paw impatiently above the next step.

"How?" I ask.

The old man begins to open his mouth.

"No. Never mind." And I drop my finger to signal the attack.

The first one is on him immediately and, sensing easy prey, the others follow. They tear through his flesh and his piercing screams do provide some satisfaction. I am not an evil person, but what I have been through would turn anyone.

Even as his skin is ripped off, unveiling white bone and glistening tissue, he is conscious, and his legs continue to kick redundantly. I can only imagine the amount of pain he feels. And it will never be enough.

It is only when one of them bites at his throat that his physical body finally quits its struggle. The screaming continues, though, as they pull his soul from its bloody, broken shell and take off with it back through the hole to wherever it will spend eternity.

I could never understand the need for closure that victims of loss craved. I used to think if they were gone, they were gone. But some peace has found me now. Details of his death would only torment, so l choose to remember him for who he was: a ray of sunshine that warmed every minute of my existence.

I walk up the steps without looking back, unable to entertain the thought that this dingy hole was the last place he saw. As I push open the front door, it is ripped out of my hand by the wind I cannot feel. The crows have disappeared, and there is no sign of the red-eyed hounds.

The sound of children laughing comes from somewhere close by, and I follow the noise around the house to find Oscar and his new friend, the boy from the clipping, playing tag in the back yard.

Finally, I allow the tears to come.

I have read that suicide is considered blasphemy. I guess even the devil has a heart.

The hounds will come back for me soon, but I am ready now.

Five Years

With headlights off and through the rain-lashed windscreen and blackness of the night, Don didn't see the tree across his side of the road until he was nearly upon it. He put his foot hard on the brake and instinctively yanked the steering wheel, sending the car fishtailing until it spun out from his control. He continued to wrestle with the wheel but couldn't even see where the road was anymore. Finally, the tyre caught the edge of the ditch.

As Don braced for impact, he found himself back in his rusty old Ford with Christine, the stereo pumping out a tune from their special road trip cassette. A loud crunch catapulted him forwards and, in a blink, the vision disappeared as the seatbelt jolted him back into the darkness again.

He unclenched his hands from the steering wheel, switched off the engine and turned to look over his shoulder. The headlights that had been on him for the last forty kilometres slowly came to a halt and the engine quieted to a gentle hum—then nothing but night.

The only sounds Don could hear were the relentless thrashing of the rain and his own laboured breathing. He removed his seat belt and threw open the driver side door. The smell of the night rushed at him, and the rain felt intensely hard and cold as he began his sprint into darkness.

There was no way to know where he was or where he was heading. Initially, his only thought had been to drive away his staring-at-the-ceiling insomnia. Now, though, it was simply to get away from the mysterious black vehicle that had relentlessly pursued him along rain-drenched roads and already rammed him twice from behind.

For the first time he could remember, he began to cry, not in fear for his life but the solitude he felt at that moment. There was nobody out there who would care if he was dead or alive.

As he ran, Don considered the vehicle that had slammed into him: unidentifiable, black with tinted windows. It had no plates. The front of the car sported a huge snarling grille. In blind fear, he had put his foot down and hoped the pursuer would eventually give up the chase.

Exhausted, he stopped running and climbed over a barrier into the foliage on the embankment. He used the branches and trunks of trees to traverse down to the bottom and sat behind one of the larger ones. The coldness returned as he watched small wisps of his breath disappear into the void.

The rumble of an engine came into earshot, but this time no headlights to give away its location.

His hunter had gotten serious now. The games were over.

Don nestled into the back of the tree as though trying to drive his way through the bark. He inhaled deeply and held his breath in case the condensation clouds gave him away.

As he heard a car door open, there was a moment of clarity that manifested itself like a kick in the gut. For a moment, he thought he might vomit; he put one hand to his mouth and closed his eyes. As if to validate the epiphany, his mind threw him back into the old Ford again with Christine. Seatbelt off, leaning over the dashboard, she snorted coke, flicked her head back and smiled before turning the rear-view mirror to herself to wipe the dust from her nose.

Christine sprinkled the last of the powder across her wrist and held it out for him, and as Don leaned in, the car drifted lanes and collided with the truck that had been approaching at speed.

He could still remember the explosion of noise and the sound of metal on metal as the vehicles momentarily melded together. And then Christine began to fly. Her body was tossed as the car flipped over and shards of glass showered everywhere as her head was sent violently through the windscreen. He remembered her dead eyes and her bloody broken face vividly.

The police found a half-empty six-pack on the truck driver's passenger seat. Don told the police the truck came out of nowhere and knocked them off the road. It was too easy.

The guy was sent down for five years in '75.

Perhaps with parole? It must be him!

Since Christine died, Don had alienated himself from everyone, not feeling worthy or capable of companionship. The guilt and grief had almost devoured him, and every day was an effort. Sometimes he wished he had told the truth. Maybe then he'd have had closure.

As he sat behind the tree in his cold, wet clothes, he contemplated how long he could keep running. The guy had been waiting over three years to get his revenge; he wasn't going to let up. But perhaps if he saw the grief and remorse in Don's eyes, there might be another way.

"Hey," he called, "I'm coming up to talk."

He scrambled up the side of the embankment and found two shiny black boots waiting for him. The silver skull on each tip was the last thing Don saw as the iron bar smashed into the side of his face.

The man bent down to grip Don's collar and then dragged him along the wet tarmac. He opened the boot of his car and bundled him next to another body.

After closing it, he lit a cigarette and drove off into the darkness to find his next victim.

The Paperboy

Somewhere in England, 1984

As he hoisted the orange bag full of newspapers onto his shoulder, twelve-year-old Jake felt an enormous sense of pride. He was about to start his first proper job. It was an opportunity to earn money that wouldn't be coming from the pocket of his parents for second-rate efforts at washing up and keeping his room tidy. He lifted his bike from the driveway and looked back to the house to see his mum waving at him through the bay window, smiling broadly. He nodded back and started peddling towards Newhaven Crescent, the lucky estate that would have him as their paperboy for the foreseeable future. In five weeks, he'd be able to buy the new top of the range Transformer. With some extra jobs at home, perhaps sooner.

It was a three-mile bike ride and no mean feat with a heavy bag of papers around his shoulders. By the time Jake turned into the street, he already felt a cold stream of sweat running down his back. He dismounted the bike and leaned it against the lamp post, and as he adjusted the heavy orange bag on his shoulders full to the brim with newspapers, he heard a voice call out, "Young lad, are you our new paperboy?"

Jake lifted his head to see the white-haired old lady standing in the doorway of Number One, and a thousand smart-arse answers filled his head, but he politely replied, "Yes."

"Oh, goody, we've been expecting you. It's been four years since the last one!"

His dad had taken him around in the car on Sunday night, and it turned out Newhaven Crescent was a retirement village, full of perfectly manicured lawns and dull pebble-dashed houses. Thankfully, they hadn't come across any vicious hounds of hell, just an extraordinary number of black cats. The place had been eerily quiet, without a single person walking around or pottering in the garden or even twitching at the curtains. His dad had said they were all probably at a community event or bingo or perhaps at sundown they all shapeshifted into cats.

After neatly folding the paper, he walked towards the old lady and handed it over. Old people always seemed like an alien species to him. They were obviously human, but communication with them was limited, and he always felt slightly uncomfortable in their presence.

They were nice enough—sometimes grumpy—but he found it hard to believe they were young once, as though all the fun stuff had been syphoned away over time. And they all smelt like TCP and cough drops.

She smiled and, in return for the newspaper, handed over twenty pence.

"Thanks, but I already get paid for this," he said.

The old lady's breathing seemed fast and erratic—not awkward, but excitable—and he noticed that since arriving she had not taken her eyes off him.

"The name is Joan. It's good to meet you, Jake. Call that a bonus."

As he was about to ask how she knew his name, another voice from across the road shouted, "New paperboy?" and he looked across and saw the door to Number Two wide open, and an elderly gentleman beckoning him over.

"Thanks, Joan," he said and took the coin before making his way across the road.

As he reached the path of the old man, he looked back towards Joan's house and saw that she was still watching him from the doorway. She quickly shut the door behind her; almost immediately, the curtains twitched.

The old man's face looked about two hundred years old, with bits of hair erratically shooting from his nostrils and ears, and his eyebrows looked as though they were trying to escape across the side of his face. He was dancing, doing a little jig. He wasn't Michael Jackson, but he had some moves, Jake mused.

"Wonderful, wonderful. It's been so long!"

Jake held out the paper, and the old man made to grab it and then snapped his hand back and laughed. He repeated the sequence three more times before finally clamping his misshapen fingers around the newspaper and snatching it away. The old man planted his other hand on top of Jake's head and ruffled his hair, a gesture Jake always hated, and even more so when he went to straighten his hair and felt the sticky dampness that remained.

He retreated and smiled and, once he was back onto the pavement, he saw that the entire street now had their front doors wide open, with each of the occupiers standing on the doorstep ready to greet him. Some of them danced excitedly in their doorways.

Number Three was an old gentleman called Harry, and in exchange for the newspaper, he had given Jake a ten pence coin. When Jake reached for the reward, the old man had bent down and whispered in his ear, "Get as much fanny as you can, lad."

Jake nodded and slowly retreated down the path. He didn't know what to do with that information; the closest he got was the underwear section of his mum's catalogue, so he decided to bank that little pearl for another day.

Number Four was a blue rinse named Edith, and she invited him in for a soda and cream bun. He thought he must have been given the luckiest street in town as he wiped the cream moustache away and glugged some of the soda down. And even though it tasted flat, he let out one almighty burp and immediately put his hand to his mouth. The old lady looked at him and cocked her head from side to side.

"Sorry, excuse me," he said.

She started laughing then, a gentle giggle at first, but then it cranked up a few notches to a full-blown roar, and before long she was rolling on the floor clutching her belly and guffawing so hard she had tears in her eyes.

The subsequent and again involuntary burp from Jake sent her over the edge. Struggling to breathe through her raucous laughter, she started to cough violently and profusely, and then suddenly her teeth shot out across the wooden floor. This only caused more hysterics. Jake guessed it was a good five minutes before she finally composed herself and collected her dentures.

"Sorry, Jake, I'll just pop to the bathroom. I think a bit of wee came out."

With his opinion of old people upheld, he drank the rest of the soda and went through to the living room to take a look around. An old Grandfather clock stood in the corner, ticking loudly. Standing next to it was an old cupboard crammed full of teapots and teacups, and a wooden thimble holder bristled with shades of green and pink just above it. Near the huge overflowing basket of wool and knitting needles, there were some old photographs on a table. Jake assumed them to be of Edith's family. The balloons indicated it was her ninetieth birthday party, and there were people of various ages crowded around her chair and smiling into the camera. He glanced out the window briefly and saw the old people still patiently waiting in their doorways, and thought he better get a move on if he wanted to make it back before midnight.

As he made his way back to the kitchen, he noticed some old newspapers on the bottom tray of the centre table, and he squatted and pulled the first one towards him.

"I won't be long, don't shoot off just yet," the voice came from the bathroom.

The date on the newspaper was 23rd September 1980. He noted the date on his digital watch as 22nd; it was almost four years to the day since publication.

"Jake," the voice came from behind.

"Hi, I was just looking. Sorry."

It didn't register immediately, and it could have been his mind censoring the image out, but it soon hit him that she was no longer wearing any pants or underwear. She smiled intently at him, battered her eyelids and asked, "Do you want to take a photograph, Jake?"

At first, he couldn't find his words and focused his eyes on the yellowing textured swirls in the ceiling as he sidestepped back towards the kitchen. "I have to finish the rest of my round now. Thanks for the drink and cake."

She laughed then and winked, "I'm just playing with you, Jake. You can get away with anything when you're old."

He smiled, grabbed his orange bag, and made his way to the door. As he stepped outside onto the pavement, Edith shouted behind him, "See you tomorrow, Jake. It's my ninetieth, you know!"

He didn't have the heart to say anything. If she wanted to believe she would be turning ninety again, it wasn't his place to ruin that. There was a purpose to his movement now, a need to get home and to be in his room and away from the smells and idiosyncrasies of the old and the oppressive feeling the street was starting to provide.

Number Five was ready for him, a burly old lady named Janet who made him go inside for another soda and a chat after not taking no for an answer, arms of a sumo wrestler pulling him in from the lovely fresh air outside. He counted six black cats in the kitchen, but it smelt like there were more—the house offered an unholy cocktail of urine and stale perfume. Jake wanted to be out as soon as he walked in. Janet had frizzy grey hair and a bright red face, the same colour as the five stones encrusted onto the star-shaped pendant that draped from her neck.

"You look like you need filling up, boy. Give me a minute," she said and then disappeared into the pantry.

He looked around and noted the three overflowing cat litters on the floor. He wasn't sure how long he could stand there without gagging, so he shifted across to the open window. The calendar immediately caught his eye as it swayed gently in the gratefully received breeze. The 23rd September had been highlighted in red pen with the same shape that decorated Janet's neck: a star within a circle. He opened the can of cola, took a sip and then placed it back down on the counter, unable to stomach any more flat soda.

She came back with a box of doughnuts and offered him one which he accepted politely but then said he had to be on his way to finish his round. She looked disappointed as she walked him to the front door, but before he could leave, asked him to wait just one more minute. She came back with a brand spanking new Polaroid camera and took a picture of him. She smiled once the print came out.

"Perfect," she said.

She waved him off as he walked down the path and told him that Nana Ivy was looking forward to seeing him.

Thirty-five minutes had passed, and he had delivered five papers.

Number six was an old man called Geoff who collected his toenail clippings in an old lunchbox. He said he was going to leave them to Jake in his Will and then laughed. With his false teeth laid on the palm of his right hand, he proceeded to run through an old ventriloquist act that he said he often did at the community centre. Jake wanted to stay twelve years old forever.

Clementine was next—a sweet old lady that had beautiful snow-white hair. She took him through to the kitchen and offered him some candy, the type that was hard on the outside but chewy on the inside. He spent the majority of their conversation with his fingers in his mouth, trying to prize them from his teeth. She told him she was a widow and married for sixty-two years until her husband Arthur had died.

"I'll go and grab a photograph of him. Give me one second. Nana Ivy doesn't let me have them up in the house but wait there."

He looked around the kitchen and noted the calendar with the same star shape surrounding the number 23, no writing adjacent, but it was evident that something was going to happen on that date.

"Go through to the living room, darling, and make yourself comfortable."

He looked at his watch, sighed, and went to sit down on the bright orange sofa. There were pictures of Elvis Presley everywhere and a bookshelf full of photo albums of all shapes and sizes.

"Just give me a minute; I know it is here somewhere."

He took one from the shelf and started flicking through it. There were pictures of Clementine, with who he assumed to be her family, at the seaside and restaurants and various locations with people who looked of a similar age. It was all very boring. He replaced it with one in the middle of the shelf and opened it up halfway to some photographs that had someone's head cut out. One of them showed Clementine smiling and holding hands with a nicely dressed headless gentleman whom he assumed to be Arthur. He quickly put the album back and peaked through the hallway, but there was no sign of her so picked up one from the very end. As he opened it, an old black and white photograph of a baby fell to the floor. On the back of it in scrawling handwriting was written the name Clementine and the date November 1883.

"Got it," she shouted down the hallway.

He collected the photo quickly and slipped it back in the album before fumbling it back onto the shelf.

"This is the only one I have, but please don't tell anyone as they will take it away from me."

"Why?" He couldn't help himself.

"Oh, it's hard to explain, Jake. The short story is he didn't want to be part of the community anymore, and they gave me an ultimatum, him or them." She kissed the photograph then and turned to smile at Jake. "It sounds harsh, I know, but if you knew what I knew, then it would make sense."

The woman in front of him had apparently been on the planet for over one hundred years. Jack would have guessed about eighty at a shot, so she was doing something right. He thanked her for the candy and said he had to be on his way. As he left the old lady reminded him, "Please don't tell Nana Ivy."

"I won't," he said and smiled and left for Number Eight. On his visit to the next few houses he was offered chocolate and crisps; even a blowjob from Doris at Number Twenty-three. He put that one down to dementia.

Benjamin was waiting for him at Number Sixty-four, wearing an old gas mask at the doorway. It reminded him of Darth Vader and even more so when the old guy spoke in a low guttural voice, "I am your father, Jake," and laughed hysterically. He took off the gas mask to reveal a bald, olive-skinned head. His eyes pointed in slightly different directions. Forcefully, he began pushing Jake through the door and took him into the front room that was decorated wall to wall with war memorabilia. An old gun in a glass case hung above the fireplace and pictures of spitfires decorated the yellow walls. Various cupboards and tables were crammed full of plastic models of the same plane, and even one made of matchsticks took centrepiece on the coffee table in the middle of the lounge.

"Took me all day to do that one," he said as he handed Jake a can of soda.

"It's cool, Benjamin," he said, genuinely impressed.

"Call me Ben," he said and winked. "I've got more of the matchstick models if you are interested."

"Yes, please."

His new friend Ben disappeared eagerly out of the room, and Jake put the soda on the coffee table and surveyed the lounge. In the corner was an overflowing wicker magazine rack, crammed full of yellow newspapers and magazines, and the first thing he pulled out was an old TV Times from 1972 and behind it was a newspaper dated 23rd September 1980. There were some older issues shoved behind but what caught his eye was the huge red book that rested diagonally against the side of the bookcase above, an embossed circle encased a star with five points and suggested significance of some sorts. He picked up the book and opened it, and immediately the yellowed pages and stale smell gave him the impression the book was incredibly old. The words weren't English but a mixture of texts and symbols that meant nothing to Jake. There was a piece of paper sticking out of the book towards the middle, and he flicked to the relevant page to reveal the black and white print of a young boy. On the back of the picture, someone had written Tommy and the year 1980.

When Ben came back in and saw Jake looking at the book, his demeanour instantly changed.

"I think you better leave now, son. I don't like snoops."

"Sorry, Ben, I was just interested. I really want to see the models you've made."

"The name is Benjamin, kiddo." he said before snatching the book away. "Now. Off you fuck!"

There was a pause, and he half expected the old man to start laughing, but his face remained stern all the way to the front door and most likely after it had slammed shut behind him.

On his way to the next house, he collected his thoughts and assumed Tommy was someone precious to the old man, perhaps a grandson. He was disappointed, as he had been genuinely interested in the modelling and was upset that the old codger had kicked him out.

It had been one hell of a day and one hell of a welcome, and he made a note to try and start being friendly but firm. The watch indicated it was already 6:20, and he had to get on with the round; otherwise, his dad would be out looking for him. He wanted to finish the job on his own. Finally, after a few more meet and greets and exchanges of newspapers for candy and the polite refusal of umpteen cans of no doubt flat soda, he reached Nana Ivy's house.

He knew it was Nana Ivy's house as it had a plaque on the wall saying it was. The garden was full of strange objects, lots of stone frogs and gargoyle type creatures, even a small statue of what looked to be a leprechaun holding his little pickle and spraying water into a garden bed — the strangest little fountain Jake had ever seen. On the front of the glossy red door, there was a black star with a circle running around it, just like on the calendars. Three more black cats monopolised the doorstep, lounging in the evening sun. They eyed him briefly and stretched and then went back to their sleep.

He was relieved there was nobody there to greet him, and he folded the paper neatly and put it into the letterbox in the front door. Immediately it was snatched from the other side, and the door swung open, revealing a large lady with the biggest smile he'd seen all day and more jewelry around her neck than Mister T.

"Jake," she roared.

He stood dumbfounded at the door and tried to speak, but before he could, she put her big hands on his tiny shoulders and dragged him in through the front door.

"Don't be shy, boy. I'm Nana Ivy!"

"Hi," he replied sheepishly.

The hallway was abundant with all sorts of obscure art, paintings displaying the screaming faces of demons, statues of contorted figures with various limbs missing, and more of those symbols with metallic rings housing the five-pointed stars hung on the walls. Centre stage, resting on a sideboard, surrounded by a dozen or so lit candles was a black and white photograph of the entire community, all of them holding hands around the same large circular symbol.

He recognised the faces that were visible and, of course, next to Clementine was the smudged-out face of her husband Arthur, the outcast.

"Come through, boy," she insisted.

The smell of scented candles drifted through the house, but it wasn't unpleasant. As he walked through to the kitchen, even after all the candy and soda, the smell was mouth-watering.

"Do you like apple pie?"

Two pieces later under the watchful eye of Nana Ivy, he said he had to be going and thanked her a million times for the pie. She laughed it off, but before he even made an effort to get out of his seat, her big hands clamped around his shoulders once again and asserted the fact she wasn't finished with him just yet.

She went to sit in the chair opposite and then looked directly at him until he started to feel uncomfortable and shift around. "Do you like cards?" she asked.

"Yes, I play fish with my dad sometimes, and he's teaching me how to play gin rummy, too."

She took the pack from her trouser pocket, opened it, and placed the cards face down on the table. The cards were larger and looked heavier and more cardinal than others he had seen.

When Nana Ivy shooed his hand away, that was made even more apparent. She shuffled and asked Jack to pick five. He did, and she looked the cards over and nodded and then put them back in the pack.

"Did I win?" he asked.

"You win another piece of pie to take him with you tonight," Nana Ivy replied and winked.

She cut him another slice and wrapped it in kitchen roll before slipping it into his orange bag.

"Hey, young Jake, what is your favourite pie? I will cook another one for you tomorrow."

"Um, have to be blackberry, Ivy," he replied.

"Nana Ivy!" she corrected sternly.

"Sorry, Nana Ivy."

She smiled and patted him on his head, "Good lad. I will have one ready for you tomorrow."

He said goodbye and walked back to collect his bike. Even though there was urgency in his step, he could still make out the twitching curtains as he walked by the houses. Once he sat in the saddle, he gave one last look back and saw what looked to be the entire street staring back at him from their lounge room windows. He shivered and sped off into the evening and back to his home where nobody was over the age of fifty.

As soon as he got back to his house, he let his Raleigh Grifter fall to the ground on the front lawn and rushed up the front steps. He'd never paid much attention to the Home Sweet Home welcome mat before, but tonight he had to agree. In the kitchen, his mum and dad were eating dinner.

"I was just about to come and get you, champ," said his dad.

"I know—sorry," he said and then sighed. "Old people." He shook his head.

His mum and dad laughed, and then his mum said, "We're proud of you, Jake."

"Thanks, Mum."

"So, how was it?" his dad asked.

"It was fine," he replied. "I'm beat now, though."

"There's spaghetti in the pan. You'll need to warm it up, and there are two slices of cold toast on the side," his dad replied. "We didn't realise you'd be so long. What kept you, anyway?"

He thought about telling them for a second but decided he didn't have the energy, and besides, he wouldn't know where to begin. Would he lead with the eviction from the old fart's house or the lady who wee'd herself and then asked Jack to take a picture of her privates, or would it be the sexual favours promised by Number Twenty-three?

"I'm actually not hungry. Can I go to my room?"

"Sure thing, boss," his dad said softly. "Are you okay?"

"A bit tired." His feet were very sore, but his stomach was doing somersaults from the epic amounts of candy and cakes he had destroyed.

Once upstairs, he sat at his desk, opened the catalogue to the page with the corner folded over and admired the shiny metallic Transformer. There was a huge sense of achievement as he wiped one of the lines from the tally on the chalkboard above his desk; only another twenty or so days and he'd be able to buy it outright and with his own cash. He took the magazine onto his bed. It was good to rest his weary feet. His stomach soon began to settle, and before long he was fast asleep.

***

It was time again, homework done, and day two of his paper round. The plan was simple: pass and move. Don't engage. Be friendly but intentional.

He leaned his bike against the same lamppost as the day before and looked to the street ahead. No movement at all, just like the day his dad had driven through the area. There was no sign of twitching curtains, and no eager old people jigging up and down impatiently. It was like a ghost town.

With first newspaper in hand, he made his way to Joan's house, half expecting the door to fly open as he approached. He kept his eyes on the bay window as he walked down the path, watching for any signs of movement, and even after pushing the paper through the letterbox and his hasty retreat down the path, he hadn't thought he'd get away with it.

On to Number Two, and the old guy with the sticky hands and the two furry friends that lived above his eyes, but again, no twitching curtains and no sign that anyone was home. Number Three was the same, and no sign of pissy pants at Number Four. The thought crossed his mind that he could be finished in twenty minutes — without trauma. He ran from house to house, expertly rolling the papers and threading them through the letterboxes without a single encounter.

He took the last paper from his bag and walked down the path to Nana Ivy's front door. On the welcome mat outside was a plate with a slab of pie and next to it was a little piece of paper with his name scrawled on it. On the back was written "blackberry pie."
The aroma was amazing, a heady cocktail of summer fruit and sugary pastry and, even after the pig-out the day before, Jake felt immediately ravenous. He put the empty orange bag down, sat on the doormat and scooped the pie up to find it freshly warm from the oven — or at the very

least recently reheated. The fluffy pastry caved, and the deep richness of the fruit exploded into his mouth. It was heavenly. In his twelve years on the planet, he had never tasted anything as exquisite, and he felt extremely disappointed as he put the last piece in his mouth and licked his fingers. He picked up the bag and made his way back towards his bike.

He had only walked a few steps back before he realised the bike was missing, no longer leaning against the lamppost where he left it. His pace quickened as panic set in at the thought of the long walk back home and the fact his dad would go nuts as the bike was only a few months old. He'd had visions of being home well before six with ample time to watch TV and play.

He made it about halfway down the street before the world started spinning, and his legs gave way. As he fell to the ground, he managed to put his hands out in time to avoid a face full of tarmac. His body felt heavy, as did his eyes, and, all of a sudden, he was completely exhausted. As he let his face rest against the ground, the houses started to swim around but were quickly flooded away by a river of darkness.

***

Chairs scraped across the floor and loud and urgent voices surrounded him. His head pounded. As he slowly opened his eyes, he began to recognise the familiar faces of Newhaven Crescent busying around in what he assumed to be the community hall in preparation for something. The chairs were all facing his direction.

He tried to get up but realised he was bound to the chair with what looked like a mile of yarn, and as he clumsily bucked to and fro, he saw the star on the ground in front of him and the familiar ring that circled it. There was a lit candle on each point of the star, and in its centre were black and white prints of two young boys with the word missing in bold text on the bottom of each poster. On one of them, he made out the name Tommy. Jack recognised him as the boy from the photograph that had slipped out of the heavy red book. He then saw the smaller photograph of himself, the one that Janet had taken, in between the two larger ones.

"How long have we got?" a voice asked.

"We managed to keep him over an hour yesterday. Don't worry, we have plenty of time," someone replied.

The drum started then, and people began to take to their seats. The pain in his head synchronised perfectly with the beat to make the effect even more dramatic.

He looked towards the audience and saw Edith, the birthday girl, with the balloons tied to her chair. She smiled and waved at him. There was a buzz of excitement as the old people chatted and waited for further direction.

A strange smell, a sort of sickly-sweet burning, started to waft towards him. It wasn't long before the source became apparent. Nana Ivy came running through the door, completely naked, and holding out in front of her some plant or herb that was smouldering away. She was chanting in a language Jake didn't recognise, and he guessed it was the strange text that he'd seen in the embossed red book. Each member of the audience started to embrace her and, once she had waved the smouldering plant in front of them, they bowed and kissed her feet. She headed for Jake then and danced around him, her breasts bounding only inches away from his face in a violent pendulous motion. He closed his eyes and winced as she came up close and kissed him on the forehead.

"Let's hear it for Jake, everybody," she shouted.

The hall filled with applause and a few whistles. Someone heckled "Snoop," and he didn't need two guesses on that one. Once the applause died down, Nana Ivy walked into the centre of the circle, knelt down, and kissed each of the photographs.

Jake was terrified. Something big was going to happen, and it appeared he was the main attraction. He missed his mum and dad and wanted to be home. He felt the first tear run down his cheek.

"Jake, please don't cry," Nana Ivy said. "This is your destiny. We have been waiting so long, and the cards never lie."

"I want to go home," he whimpered, finally managing to find some sort of voice.

"Jake, take some comfort from the longevity you are going to provide this beautiful community. Our pact with our good Lord Satan will ensure we will all be rewarded with the last four years of our lives in return for yours."

He started to sob then, uncontrollably. It had to be some sick joke. The word "Please" left his lips.

"Jake, we are a community, and we look out for each other, and sometimes we have to do drastic things to protect ourselves. We are part of something strong, and in the last twenty years, we have only lost one person. Perhaps it would be more appropriate to say that he lost his way," she turned her head and winked towards Clementine. "This ritual allows us to continue in our group and thrive, and, by offering young blood, we can gain extra time we wouldn't normally have. Most of us in this room are over a hundred earth years old."

She put her hand on Jake's cheek and wiped away the tear. "It's time," she said.

Nana Ivy walked across to the other side of the room and disappeared out of Jake's vision. When she came back, she was wearing a demonic mask like the one Jake had seen in her hallway and carrying a plate with a piece of the pie. The combination of the two large horns protruding from the top of the forehead and the blood red painted eyes was more than Jake could take. He started screaming and rocking back and forth. He was foaming at the mouth as he threw himself around in desperation.

She reached behind her back and pulled the large knife out.

The drumming started again, and then Nana Ivy leaned in close and held the piece of pie out to Jake. "Its best you eat more pie now, Jake," she whispered in his ear.

The dampness was immediate, and he felt the warmth creeping across the front of his shorts.

A voice shouted across the room, "See, even young folk piss themselves," and he knew it was Edith.

Nana Ivy placed the blade against his neck and leaned in once more, "It really is best if you eat the pie now, Jake."

He took a bite. It was still good, somehow. Even with death looming and mixed with salty tears, it still tasted so goddamn good.

"Do you want a quick blowjob as a last request?" Doris piped up and removed her teeth to make a smacking sound with her lips. The hall filled with raucous laughter.

Jake slowly began to slip into darkness as the crowd began singing Happy Birthday to Edith.

His last thoughts were of his family and the stupid transformer toy he wished he'd never seen.

The Devil and the Deep Blue Sea

I'm convinced that I'm going to die. My arms are aching, and I have swallowed mouthfuls of water. I can no longer see the shore or hear the noise from the holiday-makers.

The waves are lumpy and attack from all directions. The cyan translucency of the water near shore has been replaced with opaque darkness that threatens unfathomable depth. Suddenly I am under again—back in a world of darkness, disoriented, heart pounding and with an inexplicable urge to inhale, to end the struggle. But then I see the light and kick hard. Every cell in my body is screaming for oxygen as I continue the seemingly endless ascent towards the sun. I see something then, a black blur in the distance. It's impossible to make out, but it's enough to create urgency and to deplete my oxygen levels further.

My arms and legs are leaden, but the thought of Jodie telling the kids that I'm no longer around fills me with immeasurable sadness.

No. Today is not the day.

My head feels as though it is going to explode at any moment, but I continue to thrash desperately at the water. If I can just hold on. It's too late, though. I can hold my breath no longer, and the cold saltwater begins to rush into my nostrils and mouth. Just as I'm about to give in, I feel sunshine on my face, and even through the painful and violent rasping, I am filled with relief. Liquid leaks from my nostrils and I cough up as much saltwater as I can. My chest feels raw, but for now, I am still alive. I have a chance.

Squinting at the shimmer across the ever-changing meringue-like surface of the ocean, I look for a landmark. But I see only sky and ocean. *How far have I drifted?*

I felt the rip immediately. All I could do was conserve my energy and let it take me. Minutes before, I had been in the water with the kids, chasing them around and laughing. That doesn't seem as though it happened today. It feels distant, along with all my other memories.

Why did I go back out?

Jodie even shouted after me to stay between the flags, but I've been swimming for years. That rip was unnaturally strong, though.

An approaching wave threatens to break on top of me. I try to relax and control my breathing, but my chest still feels on fire. It's a big bastard, and it's getting close. I have got to get this right. I thrust myself into the blackness again, but even under the blanket of water, the power of the breaking wave sends me somersaulting downwards. Finally, an eerie silence falls, and I begin to look for the light. But I have no idea which way is up, and I am struggling for breath already. The pressure on my lungs is unbearable. This is it. There will be no last-minute reprieve, no miraculous rescue. Icy-cold water begins to cascade through my nostrils and mouth, pain surges through my entire body; it feels like someone is injecting me with poison. That shape again. It's drawing closer. I'm starting to feel dizzy. The pain is subsiding along with any hope of getting out of this alive. A single bubble leaves my lips towards the surface, and, finally, the black shape reveals itself. With a silent internal scream, my world washes away.

***

My eyes open to an immense bright white light—momentarily disturbed by a sinister patch of darkness that passes over me. But soon I am squinting away from the sun, and I see the audience of concerned faces. When I spot Jodie, pure exhilaration courses through my body.

I urgently push myself up. Immediately, I know something isn't right. Nobody rushes towards me, there are no murmurs from the crowd, and they continue to stare at the sand where I once laid.

Suddenly, from behind, I can hear someone coughing and spluttering, and I turn to see my pale body convulsing water onto the sand. Two lifeguards squat either side. One of them is shaking as he brings the defibrillator back towards his chest. He smiles through watery eyes but reasserts his 'all in a day's work' nonchalance. "Thought you were a goner, mate!"

Jodie walks towards me and passes straight through my body. Her eyes are red and raw. Helplessly, I watch as she leans in towards the stranger on the sand and kisses his forehead. The other lifeguard is telling me to rest and not to move, that emergency services are on their way. The applause begins, and there are some whistles, too. I feel so cold—more so than can be attributed to the sun disappearing behind the cloud.

"That isn't me, I'm here," I scream. But nobody looks.

As the sun re-emerges, I squint to see my children standing behind Jodie. They force smiles as she turns to them. I notice the tall man standing to their left. I've never seen him before, yet he is looking directly at me. He walks over and stops only a few feet away. His face is pale, almost translucent, skin impossibly smooth, and the eyes are pitch black spheres with no pupils, no whites to be seen. With complete neutrality, he says "Condolences, dude. Ain't no happy endings here."

I turn to watch as the entity continues to reanimate my dead body. There is a noticeable dark aura attaching itself that begins to swirl menacingly.

"Took me two years ago," the man says. "People think the devil is not of this world, but he lives down there in the darkness of the water."

He begins to walk towards the ocean. "You better say a prayer for your family."

My skin suddenly begins to tighten. I am losing hair everywhere and the colour is draining from my vision.

I hear the ocean calling.

Bloody Dogs

It is another day in suburban Hell, and the grey of the sky only sets low expectations. Dogs bark at nothing at all—perhaps to only communicate their boredom to each other. This town has no future, only a fading past.

Arnold sits at the front of his crumbling house, lonely and hoping someone passes by so he can start a conversation about the weather or the pesky dogs, but only a young kid with long hair scoots past on a skateboard. The newspaper is a distraction from the weed-infested path he had some intention of sorting out today. Edith would never have let him get away with letting the house degrade in such a way. But she isn't here anymore.

On the front page of the paper, he recognises all three of the chubby residents locking arms in front of the Anne Boleyn, the old pub at the end of the street that the council wants to tear down. They are all red in the face, giving the illusion of anger, but the last time he saw Greg, the bloke in the middle, he got a full-blown account of his troubles with high blood pressure. Liz and Betty are also on the unhealthy side of the spectrum, and most likely just enjoying time in the limelight.

Jenny is tending to her hanging baskets. She's talking to her Begonias, updating them on the gossip—mainly about the pub that George used to drink in. The conversations with her flowers started when he died. Until that point, she hadn't realised how much she prattled on. "Poor George," she thought.

She still carries an element of pride about having the neatest house down the street, only slightly tarnished by the graffiti on the side fence. But there isn't much for the kids to do around here.

She wished the bloody dogs would shut up, though.

David is on his skateboard, but there are too many cracks in the pavement to get decent momentum, so he flicks it up into his right hand. He's already late for school, but that's okay; the teachers don't run to time either. He's daydreaming about being a famous writer again but is suddenly snapped back into reality by a German Shepherd that throws itself furiously against a nearby wooden gate. He lets out a nervous laugh and speeds up. He can see the wood is breaking away from its posts, and it won't be long before it's down. Within seconds, the dog launches another attack on the fence and continues its bark, but its ferocity is soon lost in the chorus of yaps that echo around the estate.

Patricia is on the verge of tears. She stares out through the yellow net curtains and reminisces about the old days. Residents were so fastidious about their houses and gardens, so proud to part of this community, but once the money moved out, it all went downhill—just another old mining town with nothing to show but an endless chorus of barking. And then she sees the dog turd on the nature strip, and it's all too much, and the tears come. *Bloody dogs.*

Terry empties the ashtrays in the small beer garden area and collects the empty crisp packets that people have shoved down the hole in the tables. He thinks it's funny how everyone starts drinking when word gets out the pub is set to close. Takings were up again last night, but it's too little too late. Besides, the place needs more money spent on it than he has.

"Shut up, Barney, for Christ's sake," he shouts across to his Rottweiler that has been barking persistently since dawn. He grabs the broom handle from behind the bar and prods it where the sun doesn't shine, but the dog doesn't waver and continues its raucous anthem.

The bark of the dogs is becoming louder, more intense. It started earlier than usual and has been relentless since. They are all at it today—communicating, warning—but it's a case of cry domesticised wolf. Their alerts fall on ears that are well-practised in tuning out.

Arnold lifts his head from the newspaper and is immediately transfixed by the sky. It is no longer a dull grey but a swirling kaleidoscope of light and dark shades. The air suddenly feels heavy and there is a feeling of unpredictability that both excites and scares him. The hairs on the back of his neck begin to prickle and a spike of adrenaline forces his body into an involuntary shudder.

Patricia is staring at the sky. In her right hand, the dog turd gently sways between the two ends of kitchen roll, but her disgust is on hold as the swirling shades of grey provide a mesmeric effect. The first speck of rain falls on her nose and she slowly retreats inside. "Storm brewing," she whispers to herself and, with a little bit of excitement, slides the net curtains open with the hand that isn't holding the poo.

David is sprinting now. The dog scared him, but it's more than that—he feels a sense of foreboding, something in the air. The slight breeze that brought the first snap of Autumn has abruptly stopped and there is now an eerie stillness.

As she steps down from the small ladder, Jenny catches sight of David as he rushes past. She's still pretty sure he was responsible for the graffiti; he has a skateboard, after all.

"Now, then, would you look at that," she says to the Begonias as she looks up to the sky and eyes the single streak of pink that has now developed across its centre.

Terry takes a cigarette break and sits at one of the wooden benches outside. He's got one of his migraines coming—no doubt from all the barking. *Bloody dogs.* He brings the lighter to his lips but doesn't ignite; the sky suddenly demands his attention. He's never seen anything like it: thick swirls of red, like strawberry syrup, run through the milky greyness, slowly pulsating and bringing the sky to life.

The first drops of pink rain splatter across the top of his newspaper, but Arnold doesn't move. The hypnotic rhythm and swirls of red veins that are forming in the sky have him completely entranced. Even when the rain turns crimson, he remains.

Jenny is still talking to her baskets. It's only when the first drop of scarlet runs down the venation of one of the leaves that she cranes her neck back to look up. The sky is three-quarters red and bloody rain falls everywhere. It's mid-morning, but it feels more like dusk. Some of the rain patters against the top of her head and begins to run down the side of her face. "Holy shit," she says to the Begonias as the kid carrying his skateboard sprints past.

Red rain falls around him as David rushes back home with head down. He is nearly out of the street when suddenly the ground begins to shake and the pavement starts to crumble in front of him, stopping him dead in his tracks. The existing cracks become wider, more menacing, and tarmac begins to break off and fall into the dark void below. His first thought is a sinkhole. He's read about them just popping up in random places and swallowing everything around. But then he sees the hand emerging from the hole, sizzling and smoking, as though it has just been extinguished by the cool Autumn air. He wants to take a step back, but suddenly his legs feel like jelly. He wills them to move away from the perfectly manicured hand that gropes around the tarmac, but they're useless to him right now.

Terry stands in the archway leading out from the beer garden. The rain is lashing down and he can see rivers of red flowing into the drains. He holds his hand out to catch some of the drops, and the rain does not simply splash and ricochet off as expected. It is viscous—like blood. He lifts his fingers to his mouth and flicks his tongue out. The bitterness hits him straight away, a harsh metallic flavour that delivers nostalgic flashbacks of falling off bikes and scraped knees. It is undoubtedly blood.

The dogs are howling in unison now. The sticky rain mats down their fur and prevents their hackles from bristling with alarm. They are pacing up and down in the small confines of their gardens. Helpless.

Gordon is also pacing up and down his living room carpet, muttering "apocalypse" as the static noise of the television fizzes away in the background. It's been like that for over two hours now. Last week he saw a documentary about doomsday preppers and thought they were all bonkers, but the sky is bleeding outside, and he hasn't a clue what to do. Margaret is in the bath upstairs completely oblivious. *Probably best.* He hears the kettle boil so at least he has a distraction now. He will take her up a cup of tea and sit with her—just in case.

Patricia is alternating between observing the sky and the kid at the end of the street. The road is moving—breaking up—and the kid is just standing there. "Fuck," she utters as she puts on her slippers and dressing gown and lumbers down her path. "Hey, get out of the way," she shouts as she throws the poop back on the nature strip and heads towards him.

Jenny watches Patricia as she speeds by in her slippers. "Patricia," she shouts, but no response. She steps down from the ladder and follows her down the street. And then she sees the kid looking down towards the small hole in the ground and the hand reaching out from where it shouldn't. Steam is rising from the ground, and she doesn't like it one bit.

Arnold hears a woman's voice further down the street and, already sodden, decides to investigate. As he steps out from behind the overgrown hedge that lines his driveway, he sees the two old dears tottering down the pavement. He sets off after them looking like an extra in a zombie film as he drags his arthritic left leg behind him. Out of the corner of his eye, he notices the twitching curtains of the other residents but knows they have zero intention of exploring beyond the safety of their living rooms.

"Over here," Terry shouts and beckons the gathering crowd. He sees the hand, too, but has no intention of stepping outside the archway.

The voice of the pub landlord snaps David out the trance, and he hears someone approaching from behind. *There is an actual hand poking out of the road.* And then he sees the hat.

Patricia grabs the boy by the arm and begins to drag him away from the hole. Finally, Jenny catches up, and all three of them begin their slow retreat towards the Anne Boleyn.

Arnold can see the large hole in the ground now and can make out what looks to be the top of a trilby hat and someone's shoulders emerging. "Are you okay? Did you fall in?" he shouts as he drags his leg behind. In the distance, Jenny and another lady he recognises—the name escapes him— are backing away towards the pub. The skateboarder is with them, too.

"Did you see what happened?" Arnold asks the group, but they do not answer and continue their retreat. "Terry, what happened?" he shouts across to the landlord.

"Arnie, run! Get over here quickly!" Terry replies.

The guy in the trilby is nearly halfway out; the collar of his trench coat clearly visible now. The tarmac continues to melt and crumble around him.

Human voices are audible and as he slowly lifts his head for the first time, he sees one of them approaching. It is cold here. It will be a short reunion.

Even with the raucous howling all around, Arnold hears the warning from Terry but chooses to ignore it. He makes his way towards the broken tarmac and to help his fallen comrade—it's in his blood: no man left behind.

"Arnie, no!" another warning from Terry.

About ten feet from the hole, Arnold watches the trilby begin to lift. The patter of the thick bloody rain seems impossibly loud on the rim of the hat. Some of it bounces off; some of it doesn't and instead slowly begins its treacly descent and finally drips down onto the raincoat. *Good call on the jacket,* Arnold thinks. "Jeez, how the hell did you—" he begins, but the question goes unfinished as the man lifts his head. The face is human, and at first sight handsome in a yesteryear kind of way, but the eyes monopolise the face, and the other features wash away against the two blood-red orbs that exude only evil.

Finally, Arnie takes heed and begins to sidestep around the hole towards the others. The fiery eyes trace every step, and there is now an urgency in the way Arnie moves. The others are waiting in the archway for him, and he is sure they are calling him, but only the howls of the dogs reverberate in his head. Everything else is lost, and once again, he is taken back to the field—the aftermath of an explosion—blood-soaked colleagues and the interminable ringing in the ears. Disoriented, he stumbles and falls to the ground.

Terry watches his friend collapse in a heap and immediately rushes towards him. "Fuck's sake," Patricia utters as she follows. Jenny and David exchange a glance that endorses more than two would be a crowd.

Arnold can only watch in fear as the stranger slowly continues to heave himself out of the hole. His torso seems endless, and then the legs come. Finally, the visitor stands in front of him—more than eight feet tall at a guess. He cuts a sinister figure against the backdrop of the blood red sky.

The raincoat stops perfectly at his kneecaps and gives way to everyday grey slacks and the shiniest black shoes Arnie has ever seen. He cannot help but be impressed—hours of buffing his own boots back in the day would never bring out such a finish.

Gordon's cup is shaking violently in his hand and tea is spilling over the edge. "What's wrong, dear?" Margaret asks. "Nothing, dear," he says as he stares out the bathroom window at the eight-foot red-eyed giant standing at the end of their street. Gordon decides to keep this under wraps for now. She didn't sleep for a week after the stone came flying through their lounge window, and this certainly trumps that.

David feels helpless and nothing like the hero in the book he's reading. If only he could grow some balls, as his Dad put it, do something that didn't evoke disappointment. The books are all he has, his escape from the alcohol-fueled rages and constant arguments between his parents. But this is like a book brought to life, and here he is standing next to a lady who smells like bubble bath, watching the heroes from afar. He wants to rush to their aid and bring them all back to safety, but his legs won't move.

Brushing himself down, the visitor surveys his surroundings and watches the humans run towards the one on the ground. He will deal with them later, but for now: those bloody dogs. He looks towards the sky and what emerges from his mouth can only be described as a blood-curdling howl that at once silences the now seemingly pathetic whimpers. It brings with it an almighty tremor that visibly shakes the surrounding buildings.

"What was that?" Margaret asks.

"An old bomber just flew over," Gordon replies. "More tea, dear?"

The ground beneath Arnold shakes, and the already substantial hole widens further. As he feels someone grab his left arm, he watches as the tall man reaches inside his raincoat pocket and pulls out what must be an eight-inch cigar. After magically flipping the cigar into his mouth, he flicks his finger and thumb together, and an impossible three-inch flame is immediately conjured. Scrambling to his feet, Arnold cannot pull his eyes away as the stranger brings his burning thumb to the cigar and, crystal clear, he hears the leaves burn in the deafening silence that has fallen upon them.

Terry has one of Arnold's arms, and the lady whose name escapes him has the other; they are leading him back towards the pub. He was reading the newspaper only a few minutes ago, and now he is in the middle of a war zone.

Once they are through the arch, they follow Terry into the pub and watch as he bolts the door behind them. They look at each other, blood-soaked, terrified, and breathless. Nobody can bring themselves to say anything until, "Whisky?" Terry asks as he swings open the hatch and takes his natural position behind the bar.

The trilby has Patricia spooked. She recognises it for sure, even after all this time—but it can't possibly be.

From the bathroom window, Gordon watches the man blow smoke rings the size of Hula Hoops and cannot help but be impressed. After a few moments, the giant turns towards the derelict pub, removes his trilby, and runs his hand through his jet-black hair. Gordon collects Margaret's cup from the edge of the bath and heads downstairs to double bolt the front door.

Terry glances at David. "Do I know you, kid?"

"No. No, I don't think so. My dad, Frank, drinks in here a lot, though."

"Yeah, he sure does," replies Terry and pours the boy half an inch of whisky.

"What the hell is going on?" Patricia throws out the question but knows it's purely rhetorical and knocks her whisky back.

"He's coming," Jenny cries from the filthy window.

"Give me a minute," Terry says as he exits through the door near the bar. On the way out, he notices Barney quietly whimpering under one of the bar stools, a pool of what he assumes to be urine to his right.

Patricia joins Jenny at the window and offers her the tumbler of whisky. Jenny shakes her head, so she knocks it back herself.

There is no goddamn way. The trilby, the raincoat—get a grip, Patricia. The way he holds the cigar and the arrogant smoke rings chill her to the bone. She contemplates telling the others, but even the thought of it sounds ridiculous. It is just not possible.

Arnold and David join them at the window, and they watch as the stranger somehow closes forty feet in one step. A blur and then a gentle rap at the door that startles them all. He gently tips the edge of his trilby towards the window, and, with his hands nowhere near the door, the subsequent knock rattles the door violently on its hinges. In unison, they begin their retreat away from the window and back towards the bar. Terry appears from the doorway, carrying a shotgun that David immediately thinks should belong in a museum.

"Jesus Christ!" Terry utters.

"I don't think it is," Jenny replies. She surprises herself with that comment. Fear has gripped her, but this camaraderie is almost exciting. She doesn't get out the house much. Life is relentlessly dull, but this, well, this will be something to tell the grandkids about. If they make it out alive.

They scramble through the hatch and begin to line up behind Terry, hoping their scepticism about the gun is misplaced. He quickly fumbles two shells into the barrel and then snaps it back in place.

The doors are thrown open and slam loudly against the internal walls. The stranger ducks under the doorway and stands in the entrance against a backdrop of red rain and sky. *That would make a great book cover,* David can't help but think.

It's him, Patricia thinks. The eyes are different but just as evil, and he was only five-six before, but *Jesus fucking Christ, it's him!*

The group huddle together as tight as they can and, in one defensive unit, they find some comfort. The day started so normally — grey and uneventful — and now they fear for their lives. There's only Terry's antique gun between them and the eight-foot demon that has today decided to terrorise their small town.

"You move, and I shoot," Terry shouts the warning to the one who can make fire by flicking his fingers together.

"One of you knows why I am here today. I have no business with the rest of you." The voice is raspy and hoarse. The stranger takes a step forward and the doors of the pub clatter shut behind him. The gun is shaking in Terry's hand. He's only ever fired it in the sky, showing it off to his mates after a few too many. There's a lot more at stake now.

The man with the red eyes steps forward again. Terry's finger finds the trigger and rests there; he hopes he can bring himself to pull if required. Another step forward, and the trigger gives slightly under the extra pressure, but he can't bring himself to do it. "Shoot him," Patricia whispers into his ear. Another step forward.

David stands at the back of the group, still dreaming of being a hero. He crouches down and carefully places his skateboard on the ground before reaching behind his back. Relief floods through him as he feels the trusty rubber of the slingshot in his back pocket. Ten weeks of pocket money it set him back, but it was worth every penny. He could hit a can from thirty metres away with this work of art. The box of shells still sits on the table in the hallway; he places one of them in the rubber launcher.

For once, he thinks, he'll give his dad something to be proud of as he stealthily crouches behind the counter of the bar and carefully shimmies along to the far end. Finally, he reaches the hinged latch in the bar and crouches beneath it. This is his moment to shine.

Arnold and the two women inconspicuously watch his performance and whisper aggressively under their breath for him to return, but the warning falls on deaf ears, and they turn to their attention to the real danger in front of them.

"Malcolm, please. I'm coming out. I know it's me you want," Patricia says, terrified, but unable to risk anyone getting hurt at her expense.

"Malcolm?" Terry says, with more than a hint of confusion. Did she just refer to the giant demon as Malcolm?

"Stay there, Patricia," Terry shouts defiantly.

The man takes another step forward, Terry's finger instinctively wraps around the trigger, and the gun explodes. There is jolt up Terry's shoulder, and he recoils into Patricia, who shuffles back onto Jenny's toes. She stifles a yelp and steps back into Arnold's arms behind her— the closest she's been to a man since her husband died.

All eyes are on the intruder as he takes a step back and brings his hands to his chest. Terry watches him double over and sensations of relief and instant disbelief wash over him. He just shot someone.

Malcolm's shoulders start to move up and down, and for a moment, Jenny thinks he might be crying, but menacing laughter follows, and the trilby and shoulders slowly rise upward. They can only watch in silent horror as he stands and bits of metal rain down on the wooden floor. The man's lips curl upward into an awkward smile, one that reveals too many teeth, and he moves towards them purposefully.

He feels it—the adrenaline coursing through his veins—and he knows he must do something. It's his duty. Arnold rushes to the other side of the pub as fast as his crippled leg will allow and picks up a pool cue from the table. He holds it in position ready to swing and walks over to the demon. Suddenly it doesn't feel like such a good idea; his five-foot-four frame is surely not intimidating to the manifestation that stands in front of him. He swings his weapon into the giant's kneecaps, but there is no reaction—the vibration only feeds back up through his arthritic bones. The cue is snatched from his grip and, before he even has time to raise his arms, he feels the wood against the side of his face. Again. And again. The final strike sends the room spinning and he lands clumsily in a heap.

Barney growls, but it is half-assed. He remains seated under the barstool next to his puddle of piss.

Before Terry can even lift the gun up, Malcolm impossibly has the barrel of the gun in his grip. He looks towards Patricia, "This is your last chance, babe. Do you want more blood on your hands?"

"Malcolm, stop," she cries and leaves the group.

Terry tries to wrestle the gun free, but Malcolm extends his lengthy arm and wraps his fingers around his throat. The pressure is instantly excruciating, and he hears things snapping inside his neck.

"Stop," Patricia screams. "I'm coming!"

He said he would come back for her. Those were the last words he breathed out. But that was over thirty years ago. The worms should have had him by now.

She nervously walks towards him and already knows how this will end: an eye for an eye.

Terry slumps to the ground as the grip is released and the exaggerated reincarnation of her late husband turns his attention towards Patricia and smiles.

It was three decades ago, and she can still remember it as though it was yesterday, not to mention the countless interrupted nights of sleep and graphic reminders of the horrific scene that played out. No regrets, though. The bastard had it coming.

As she approaches him, his lips still curled in a menacing smile, she smells the liquor that permeates the air between them and the scene plays out in her head once more. He was in one of his moods before he left the house and came back inebriated and with a brooding evil about him. She sensed the danger immediately and tried to slip out the back door, but he got there ahead of her and wouldn't let her leave. Instead, he threw her against the wall and called her a whore. "Where are you going to go, huh?" Before she could answer, he was pushing himself against her and ripping at her dress. Her instinctive slap across his right cheek was answered with a right hook to her jaw, and she can still remember the sound of the bone cracking. But he didn't stop.

As she was doubled over the chair, he tried to lift her dress up, but she had already wrapped her hand around one of the knitting needles that poked out from the magazine rack. She didn't take one eye, she took both, and continued to puncture every other part of his body. Malcolm died a slow and painful death. And now he's back.

Patricia begins to edge tentatively towards the one she called Malcolm.

Arnold is still out cold on the floor between them.

"I've been waiting a long time for this," the hoarse voice utters. "And I finally got a day pass."

With that, he roughly grabs her arm and brings him in towards her, his eyes fixed on Terry in case he has any other ideas. The doors open on cue and he begins to drag her back into the sinister downpour outside and no doubt towards the makeshift exit that tarnishes the road like an open wound.

David takes his chance and in one smooth movement steps out from the counter and pulls back the rubber launcher. *One shot* he thinks and takes aims and releases—and prays.

Direct hit.

Malcolm feels the pain run through the entire left side of his body and immediately releases his grip on Patricia. The scream that follows is unworldly; a thousand tortured screams rolled into one. Patricia quickly runs back to the bar and into the arms of Jenny, who can feel her friend's body trembling. David grabs another shell from his pocket and loads and fires, but this one ricochets off the raincoat. *How many did I grab, was it three or four?* He reaches into his pocket and wraps his fingers around another, and feels his hand brush what he assumes to be another shell on the way out. Malcolm has recovered only slightly but begins to lumber towards him, his left hand still holding the eye that now bleeds through his fingers.

Everything has a weak spot, David thinks. He aims, fires, and the shell hurtles past Malcolm's right eye by less than an inch. David reaches into his pocket once more—Malcolm now only a few feet away—and he pulls out the boiled sweet. "Fuck," he mutters as Malcolm sweeps his hand across the side of his face and the world washes away in pain and darkness.

Jenny watches in terror as Malcolm leans over David who is now spread-eagled on the floor. She thrusts herself up, grabs a bottle of vodka from behind the bar, and makes her way towards them. Patricia wants to join her but instead begins to bawl. All of this was dead and buried, her dirty little secret—a different time and a different place. But her past just dragged itself out from a hole in the road at the end of her street.

Barney is standing now, pawing at the ground in front. He begins to bark, timidly at first, but when Malcolm grabs the kid around the throat, he finds his voice and the bark is suddenly crisp and loud. On the third yelp, the chorus of dogs begins once again. There is an urgency in their barking and the tempo is much faster than normal. Terry hears it, and the thought immediately enters his head that it's not the dogs getting louder, it's that they are getting closer.

Jenny rushes up and swings the bottle of vodka onto Malcolm's head, but the effect is only a dull thud, and the bottle doesn't even shatter. She sees David coming to and beginning to weakly grasp at the arm that has him pinned down. His face is turning bright red. In desperation, she wraps her arm around Malcolm's neck and squeezes as hard as she can, but Malcolm arches his neck forward and then brings the back of his head crashing into her nose. It snaps and caves instantly and she sees more red liquid begin to leak onto her already saturated blouse.

David is going blue, eyes bulging, and there is a pleading behind them. All Jenny can do is flail at the back of Malcolm's head and watch the poor boy's life ebb away. But then comes a scrambling noise from behind her and, before she even has time to look for the source, Barney flies past a few inches to the left of her head and clamps his teeth into the neck of the giant.

He feels it instantly, already weakened by the stupid kid's toy. He grabs at one of the hind legs and tries to yank the dog off, but its jaws remain firmly fixed around his neck. Releasing his grip from the boy, he turns his attention to the mutt and wraps his elongated fingers around its throat. Within seconds, Barney is struggling for breath, and his clutch on Malcolm finally gives.

But the first pack of dogs is already through the door and they launch at him. There is a frenzy of growls and whimpers as they snap at the limbs of their victim. Some are successful in getting through. Others are thrown against the wall, but they scramble up and re-join the pack. More of them come charging through the door, and they are on him immediately. There are too many. As soon as he brushes off one, two more pounce.

Patricia begins to regain some courage and pushes herself to her feet. She'd heard the commotion in the background, but nothing could prepare her for the sight of her giant dead husband being mauled by countless dogs, and countless more bounding in from the street. She wants to finish this once and for all—it must be at her hands; nobody else should carry that burden. Looking under the bar, she spots a small ice pick jutting out from a metal bucket, and she reaches across to retrieve it. It feels weighty in her hand, about as heavy as a good quality knitting needle, she thinks. She approaches Malcolm and nervously edges past the dogs, but they show no interest in her. Patricia watches him for a moment, helplessly struggling with the endless attack before squatting next to him with ice-pick in hand and whispering, "See you in Hell, Malcolm."

She brings it down into his right eye. The shriek is piercing.

As if summoned by the giant's scream, four large hounds walk in from outside. These are not from around here. Their eyes glow red and their coats of black matted fur sizzle and smoulder, and they are accompanied by an acrid smell of death. The smaller dogs whimper and back away as the salivating beasts make their way towards Malcolm, and the group watches, stunned, terrified, as each of the hounds grabs a limb and together remove their prey from the premises.

With their faces planted against the grimy pub window, they continue to observe as the beasts take Malcolm back into the black hole from where he appeared.

***

Another morning and, as Arnold opens his front door and stands on the step, he has never been so pleased to see the dull grey sky. After retrieving both papers from the letterbox, he sits down on his chair and waves at one of the press vans that is still parked outside. He glances at both headlines and smiles the biggest smile he has for a while: Small Town Terrorised by Eight-Foot Dead Husband. David and Goliath—the True Story. A dog barks in the distance somewhere, and his heart skips a beat. "Bloody dogs," he mutters—but doesn't mean it.

Patricia looks out her lounge window and is glad to see the grey sky. She eyes the dog poo on the front strip, but it doesn't bother her as much today. Yesterday seems like just a nightmare, and if it wasn't for the news reports on the television and the gossip from the street, she could perhaps convince herself it was. The pavements are awash with tourists, clicking their cameras at the broken road from behind the police cordon. Someone took a picture of her house this morning, too, and she didn't care for that.

Jenny is already on the steps, carefully wiping the sticky redness from her Begonias. She cannot find any words today and instead hums a tune she heard on the radio that morning. She is quite excited about going to the pub come evening, and thinks she might become a regular now there is some talk of a rescue bid from the council.

Arnold watches the news from his hospital bed; the reports mention his bravery. "Life in the old dog yet," he sniggers and performs a little salute at the television.

Margaret is reading the newspaper at the breakfast table. "I cannot believe we missed this, Gordon," she says with a sigh.

"I know love. More tea, dear?" he replies.

David sits at his study desk with the fresh writing pad in front of him. His dad is sitting in the lounge talking to two more reporters about how proud he is of his lad. He picks up the pen and writes the title for his new story: *Bloody Dogs*.

All That Glistens

He carefully balanced the fruit in the palm of his hand and enjoyed the feeling of its soft hairs against his skin. Its appearance bore some resemblance to the plum, but larger and with a distinct golden colour. It had a scent like dime-store perfume.

When he first noticed it nestled in between the other more mature fruit trees, it had looked weak and sickly and covered in a black sticky marshmallow-like substance. On one occasion, he had tried to dig it out, but the contrasting roots were huge and impenetrable, and even after dousing it with weed killer, the tree was unwilling to die. And then the first bud came.

He would not have believed it would provide such a beautiful offering, especially after producing such sinister-looking flowers— blood red freckles sprinkled across four white petals that that dangled solemnly towards the ground, and the pitch-black centre that gave off a little puff of dust when slightly squeezed.

Sometimes he stared out of the bay window observing the tree, feeling a mixture of curiosity and respect for its stubbornness to die. His wife Denise called it an unhealthy obsession, especially after finding out he had recently named the thing Veronica.

The sight of the first fruiting was an exciting time for George, and his infatuation with Veronica grew stronger. He knew for pollination there generally had to be two trees, but for the time being, he felt enormous pride in having something so special and unique in his little patch of earth.

As he closed his fist around the fruit that fit perfectly into his hand, it felt incredibly tender, as though the skin could break with the slightest of knocks. It felt ready, at its peak. He held the fruit to his nose and again the not unpleasant smell of cheap perfume wafted into his nostrils. Momentarily, the soft and warm flesh triggered an image of a firm, but pliable breast, and suddenly he felt quite aroused.

Denise stuck her head out the back door, "George, I will be at Edith's if—"

She pointed towards his crotch.

"It's—it's just pants tent," he said in defence.

She rolled her eyes. "Say goodbye to Veronica for me." She left without the usual kiss on the cheek.

He held the fruit back to his lips and felt an overwhelming urge to bite down. The scent was making him lightheaded and, as he gently rolled the fruit across his lips, his heart quickened with anticipation.

She could feel it now. It was nearly time. Even under feet of soil, she still had the power to seduce. She had no intention of staying dead; there was too much fun to be had. Over the years, roots had eventually started to form, albeit painstakingly slow, and push their way through rocks and earth towards the surface. The flowering was the easy bit—each one a previous victim—and the memories they provided were, oh, so sweet. It was the love for her husband that kept her going over the years and the hope that he was still alive.

Images of soft skin filled George's mind, accompanied by the sultry whisper of a woman inviting him to taste. He felt giddy, nervous, and absurdly weak at the knees—a feeling that brought back the memory of losing his virginity so many decades ago. His body was alive with desire and he could wait no longer.

There was a satisfying pop as his incisors sank into the silky skin and he prepared himself for the inevitable sweetness that would follow.

And he immediately knew something wasn't right. The taste that filled his mouth was unpleasantly earthy and metallic, but so greedily had he sunk his teeth in, the cold and viscous substance had already started its journey down his oesophagus.

He pulled the fruit away, and a thick string of blood and soil stretched from his lips to its underside. The untimely warm leak spread across the front of his pants as he threw the fruit on the grass and tried to retch up the grainy liquid. But it was already beginning to congeal, and suddenly he was choking. He put his hands to his throat and heard himself wheeze as he helplessly watched the small pool of blood and dirt around the discarded fruit harden and then turn to ash.

Slowly his world began to slip away.

Another victim and, for now, his body would suffice. The breeze touched her cheek, and how good it was to feel something after all this time. Vibrant colours started to form, even more spectacular than she remembered. The smells of this new time excited her, and she sensed opportunity everywhere. She counted every winter, each one an ordeal endured to bring her closer to her husband—over a hundred years under the soil—but soon, they would be reunited.

The day she set eyes on him, she knew he was the one. She sensed the innate evil and the carnage they could share. Besotted, they married and began their journey into darkness.

Intoxicated with false hope and cheap scent, the men would flock, and he would gut them. So much blood and laughter; they would feast on their hearts and lift their blood-filled glasses in a toast.

For so long, they had free rein—until the day the so-called vigilantes set their trap.

They buried her alive; laughing as they threw the earth over her face. It was the price they both paid for complacency, and there was no way they would ever let them see a trial.

With no knowledge of his demise, she could only assume he met the same fate and hoped that he, too, would be carving his way back through the earth. She had come so far with blind faith but needed his pollen to be able to fruit.

Now she knows he is close.

Jimmy Davenport

"Face your fears, Jim," my dad used to say. But he was a brave bastard, nurtured on porridge and discipline. Cancer got him in the end, unconquerable with bravado alone. I was eleven when he died, but even back then I knew he was something special, and over the years, I would feel the pressure from everyone that knew him to be the 'idea' of his son.

After guiding my foot into the next crease, I pull myself up using the tenuous grip on the rock above and, finally, I'm on level ground — about four hundred feet above the car park. To me, this will always be his mountain, the one Mum said he used to go when the dark cloud came. Today, I am borrowing it. Shrugging off the backpack, I breathe in a huge gulp of air before sinking to the ground to rest my calves. I know the hardest is to come.

Already, I feel a sense of achievement, but the ominous storm cloud that floats towards the mountain is making me anxious. And, as I crane my head towards the peak, nausea and rapid heart rate returns. Nervously, I run my fingers over the medal in my pocket, the one he got for bravery, and the one I carry with me whenever I am scared. The thumping in my ear eases a little, but not the swirling out of control sensation that has been with me since I caught sight of the mountain in my windscreen.

My father, according to his friends, wasn't scared of anything. In contrast, I was a nervous child, with an unhealthy fear of most things, and my life so far has played out to an anthem of comparison and disappointment. "Tommy wouldn't have cried." "Hard as nails 'e was." "Davenports don't shy away from a brawl." "You'll never fill his shoes!"

In their eyes, Tommy was God. And in mine, too.

I wrote the list shortly after he died. The face your fear list was the most appropriate way I could think to honour the man. And soon, at eighteen years of age, I will be able to strike the fear of heights from the list. Only one thing would remain.

As I get to my feet and brush myself down, two routes present themselves: the notoriously difficult side for seasoned professionals, and the easy side for beginners like me. My father, of course, only ever took the difficult route, and this will be my path today. "In for a penny, in for a pound," as he used to say. So, after placing my backpack against the side of the mountain, I give the medal one last rub and set off towards the peak.

It was only later, when Mum spoke of his battles with depression and anxiety, that I saw him as more human—fallible—and thus began to feel closer to him on a more emotional level. And that's a strange thing to say about a dead man. But as I stretch towards the first foothold, I know today is as much about me as it is him.

It's going well. I am getting into a rhythm, nimbly manoeuvring up the rocks and planning at least four moves ahead. It's coming so easy. But all the time, in the corner of my eye, I can see the dark cloud closing in, and its internal flashes warn of things to come. I can smell it too, the pre-storm smell—the one that still brings memories of hiding under the bed with my hands over my ears.

I make the rookie mistake of looking down then, nerves getting the better of me, and I see the mountain's sharp grey teeth ready to tear through my skin. An immediate wave of dizziness washes over me, and my breathing begins to feel less automatic as I swallow short, sharp gulps of air. For a moment, I feel as though I might pass out, and I close my eyes and grip the rock even more tightly.

A memory comes into mind. I'm a child again, standing on a bridge, watching as the white water of the river takes my stick. I recall the fear as I leaned over to watch, but also the surprising and almost overwhelming compulsion to let myself go over—the same hypnotic sensation that is sweeping across me right now. I dig my fingers deeper into the crevice and pray for it to pass. My heart is pounding—all cockiness has gone. It's just me—the one with the list—and the mountain. I open my eyes and try and regain control, but the scenery below is just a vortex of greys and greens, and it feels like it's trying to suck me in.

As I cling desperately to the rock, I see the black cloud getting closer. Number three on my list is storms—crossed out some time ago now—but watching lightning strike from the balcony of your home isn't the same as experiencing Mother Nature's fireworks on the side of an exposed mountain.

There are too many things to process, and my mind wants to shut it all out. I am not sure if my fingers are slipping or if I am losing the feeling in them. And that pull towards the ground feels so strong. As though it is meant to be.

I'm going to die.

And then I look back up the peak and see his face peering over the edge; no smile, just his stern "You've got this" frown.

"Dad?"

But I dare not release my grip on the rock. The nausea is the worst, manifesting as a tight knot in my stomach, and it hurts to breathe. Darkness is quickly falling around me as the sun is being masked by the approaching black mass, and it all feels so much more difficult. For a moment, I imagine my aching fingers losing grip and my body tumbling down the mountain, sounds of snapping and tearing until a final dull thud at the bottom.

I'm going to die—this is it!

But then my father's words echo in my head:—"Face your fears"— and a spike of adrenaline surges through my body. And I finally move my fingers, only an inch. My coordination has gone, as has my confidence. I am tentative and slow, but I force myself to keep going and, foothold after foothold, my legs start to feel sturdier and powerful again, and I work my way back into a rhythm. Finally, I make it to a break in the rock and rest.

There must be only sixty feet left, but as I look towards the peak to plan the final part of my ascent, I feel the first spot of rain and the oppressive change in the air as the black cloud digests the remaining light. The last part of the climb is steeper, and I know it is going to test me.

A bolt of lightning strikes somewhere close by, followed by a menacing roll of thunder. On cue, the rain quickly escalates from a drizzle to a downpour, and a blustery wind brings intense diagonal rain that forces me to squint. Immediately my clothes feel heavier and begin to stick to my skin, making every move more laborious.

Is this good enough, Dad?

The slippery stone provides little traction as my fingers curl around the tiny segments of protruding rock that the mountain offers. Another flash of lightning and this time the thunder is almost instant, cracking around me like cannon fire. I feel exposed as I slowly work my way up the mountain's spire-like peak. Momentum is with me, though, and rhythmically I hoist myself steadily upwards. But I see it then a few feet above—what looks to be an almost sheer piece of rock with no obvious creases or footholds whatsoever.

The woozy feeling hits me again and I'm free falling into the void.

Abruptly, a deafening growl explodes from beneath me and brings me back. My heart begins to pump faster until it pounds relentlessly in my ears. My muscles tighten, and every hair on my body prickles with terror. I have heard that noise before.

It can't be.

I look down but regret it instantly as I see the four legs of the black shape effortlessly dancing across the rocks towards me. For a moment I think I'm going insane, a combination of my mind playing tricks and the shadows of the rocks. But lightning flashes around me once again, and I see the creature in high definition: matted black fur, sinewy body, and elongated snout. Immediately I recognise it as the shape that used to live under my bed—the one on the top of my list. The one, even to this day, that still occasionally drags me from sleep, sweating and breathless.

The subsequent thunderclap explodes around me with such force it feels as though the mountain trembles, and I lose my footing. I'm hanging by my fingers, and I can feel them slowly sliding down the wet rock. Blindly, I scramble against the wall with my feet until I find footholds and, using every ounce of remaining energy, I manage to get myself back into position.

Still no visible way forward, though. I am trapped.

Drenched through, I am physically exhausted—heavy and clumsy. Mentally, I'm done.

I look down again and see the black beast watching me from what I estimate to be forty feet below. Even from here, I can see its chest heaving and muscles twitching. And as a blanket of white light crashes around us, I see its eyes for the first time: blood red, other-worldly, and holding the promise of evil. Its snout it closed, but I know there are layers of razor-sharp teeth inside ready to tear my flesh apart. I feel about eight years old again, paralysed with terror.

We study each other, fully aware of who is predator and who is prey, and slowly it sways from side to side as if waiting for me to make the first move. For what seems like minutes, we remain locked in this absurd standoff until finally, still facing the beast, I sweep my right palm across the smoothness of the rock and back again, looking for anything I can use. There it is, a crack, less than two inches in size. I lock my fingers inside and pray that my feet will find some traction. I make my move.

Momentum swings me into the rock, and my left cheek smashes against its coldness, but I am still here. Still alive. Flailing with my left hand, I find another crease that allows me to wrap my fingers around it.

And then another roar. I can even hear it panting now, and it is far too close. I drag myself up, but can't get any footing—it's too slippery, and covered in lush green moss that has no business being here.

Finally, the side of my shoe finds an imperfection in the rock, and I dig in and push myself up. Looking down, I see the beast only ten feet away. It's so close that I can see the saliva dripping from the side of its mouth, and the first sign of its jagged teeth.

Shit! Shit! Shit!

I throw my right hand out again, but nothing. I can see the top. It is only six feet away now, but the rock is too smooth, and it's not giving me anything.

A violent streak of white crackles menacingly across the oppressive black sky and blankets the mountain in light. To the right and a few feet above, I see the initials. TD. *Tommy Davenport.* And a six-inch slit in the rock.

The beast lets out a sudden roar, and I swear I can feel its warm breath. I look down and expect the creature to be reaching out towards my feet. It is.

Lightning flickers around us once more and basks the creature in a cold white radiance that frames and accentuates its malevolent red eyes. Mouth over-spilling with drool and breathing excitedly, it continues to sway from side to side, and I see every muscle on its back rippling through the matted fur. Suddenly, it cranes its head back and opens its mouth, exposing those saw-like teeth, but its roar is superseded by the explosive sound of thunder that once again vibrates through the rock as I cling to it desperately.

The beast is eyeing me again, but it has stopped swaying and is poised to strike. The excited breathing has slowed. It knows it has me. Letting go of the rock with my right hand, I dig into my pocket and wrap my fingers around the ribbon.

Face your fears.

The beast makes its move towards me, and I immediately feel small and puny—just another meal. In desperation, I swing the medal towards it with as much momentum as I can muster; it feels heavy and more weapon-like. It strikes the creature square on the chin, and the head of the beast launches back. But its claws do not give, and when it turns to me again, it growls and slashes at my leg. The pain is instant, and I feel the warmth begin to spill down my skin. I swing the medal again, but this time it just ricochets off the top of its head. Another growl, then it effortlessly scrambles up the rocks. Now it's on me, pinning me to the wet stone.

My fingers are starting to slip. I am beaten. Again that feeling of letting go swoops over me.

No! I will fight for every second. Dad would.

I am face to face with the beast that used to live under my bed. The air around is a cocktail of petrichor and rotting meat, the skin from its last meal still stuck between the sharp fangs. Its hot tongue sweeps across my face, and then it slowly inhales—savouring the delights that my flesh promises. Just as the beast recoils its head back and opens its mouth impossibly wide, I thrust my arm as far down its throat as I can. Immediately, its teeth clamp down, and searing pain screams up my arm and echoes through the rest of my body. But I see it, the realisation in its eyes as its jaws fall open and it reaches desperately for its throat. I pull my bloody arm out and watch as the beast begins to choke, releasing ugly rasps and gurgles as foam develops around its mouth. There is fear in its eyes, and I take my chance, thrusting my leg into its chest with as much force as I can muster.

"I'm Jimmy Davenport," I scream as I watch the monster fall, still clutching at its neck, eyes fixed on mine with disbelief.

My arm and leg throb with excruciating pain, raw and pulsating, and I can feel myself already growing weaker as the blood continues to leak. I am badly injured, but time is not on my side—I need to finish this. I look towards the slit in the mountain, below my father's graffiti, and ready myself. And launch. But as soon as my fingers leave the rock, I know I am not going to make it.

Instinctively, I throw my hands out, hoping they will connect with something, and for what seems like an age, they slide aimlessly down the steep slope of the mountainside. Finally, they latch on to a crease in the rock, and relief and pain wash over me simultaneously. Every nerve ending is telling me to stop moving, but I know I am fading and need to get to the top. Looking down, I scan for anything that could be used as a foothold, but when I catch sight of the endless grey below, I'm hit by another wave of dizziness. I feel so very weak now.

"Jim!" the voice floats down.

My vision is too blurry to focus, but I know he is up there, looking down at me. Squirming against the wet rock, I plant my fingers into any cavities that present themselves and, slowly and painfully, I make it to the crevice where my father's initials are etched. As I run my fingers over the letters, I begin to cry. For the days he has missed. And for the days he will never see.

Digging into my left pocket, I find a coin and scratch my faint initials beneath his—an accidental metaphor. And with one final effort that every bit of my body screams at me for making, I grab onto the ledge and pull myself up.

Even with a lacerated leg and punctured arm, nobody will believe me about the beast from under my bed that paid me a visit today. I guess it smelled the fear and wanted in. The black nemesis was the only thing left on the list. But I can cross that out now, too.

I no longer have my father's medal as a keepsake. But I do have today. He has no doubt been here with me, giving me the strength to get through this ordeal. I know that. But I also know deep down that it was me who scaled this rock, that it was me who thrust my father's medal into the throat of the beast, that it was me who faced my fears.

I am not just Tommy Davenport's son. I am Jimmy Davenport.

As I lay on my back holding my new lucky coin and watching the remainder of black cloud roll by, the first glimmer of light breaks through and illuminates the rock next to me.

"Love you, Dad."

Benedict

The smell is familiar, but not comforting: damp and putrid. It induces an overwhelming feeling of loneliness that sits heavy in my stomach. It is cold here, I can see my breath, and the drab grey walls of stone that surround me don't help.

Open manacles rest around my wrists, attached to metal chains that snake their way across to the far wall. Is this a prison? The only source of light sneaks under the door and illuminates the bowl and cup that sit beneath it on a small tray. There is a large brown rat sniffing around it.

"Oy!" my raspy voice echoes around the empty stone room. The rat carries on, uninterested.

Pushing myself from the dirty dishevelled blankets on the floor, I wince at the sudden pain that bolts down my right leg. There is a blood-soaked bandage halfway-down my thigh that I didn't notice before. I have no recollection of the injury. I don't remember anything. I have no idea who or where I am.

Suddenly ravenous, I hobble towards the door. There are etchings of the name Charlotte scratched into the stone walls that surround me. That name—where do I know that name? But soon my thoughts are clouded by a blanket of thick fog and the path to coherence is lost.

The rat scurries off into a dark recess as I bend over and reach for the food. Hungrily, I shove the cold meat in as quickly as I can, washing it down with mouthfuls of tepid water. As I place the empty cup on the corner of the sink, I note the shattered mirror above. Some of its fragments lie in the bowl, but the largest piece rests on the stone floor. Holding my thigh and grimacing, I bend over to retrieve the glass and take it over to the door. Crouching, I hold it to the light and note the dried reddish-brown stain that tarnishes the sharpest point—and for some way down.

The face that stares back is handsome but unfamiliar. I am a stranger to myself, and I wonder what kind of man wakes up in a room alone, sleeping on the floor next to such restraints.

In the sparse light, my skin looks grey; the only colour provided is from the large streak that runs three-quarters of the way down my cheek and the wound in the centre of my forehead—the same rusty hue that clings to the glass. Rotating the shard with a shaking hand, I notice the cuts that line the inside of my palm, extending to the base of the fingers. They align with this fragment perfectly.

My skin tingles with an overwhelming sense of foreboding. I feel as though I am in the middle of a dream but cannot wake up, as though I am too far gone. My body shudders involuntarily.

Who am I? What am I doing here?

With a thud, my head falls back against the iron door, and I rest it there until the world no longer threatens to wash away. There is a whirlwind of anger and frustration building inside me, and this fog is not lifting. I need some goddamn clarity. I lift my head back and throw it against the iron. The pain ricochets through my body, and it is strangely satisfying—it's all I have right now. Further back this time. And again. Again. Again.

A memory suddenly jolts in my head: the mirror. I am throwing my head against it and watching bits of my face disappear as the glass shatters. A woman is standing behind me, and her mouth is wide open in a silent scream. The glass cracks and splits her in half, and soon she is gone. All that is left is my shattered snarl. And then the memory is gone.

Who is she? I need answers.

Carefully, I slide the glass underneath the door. The reflected image provides little detail, just a flicker of light that looks inviting and in contrast to the stark darkness that surrounds me now.

I try the door and expect it to be locked, but the heavy solid gate creaks on its hinges and slowly unveils a much larger room. Directly opposite and to either side of the large timber front door, there are two windows providing a glimpse of the dullness outside and leafless trees. I have no idea what time of year it is but would guess Autumn.

A huge wooden table takes centre stage with two large chairs on either side. Four large candles sit near its centre and, in their brass holders, they flicker intensely in the invisible breeze. A small brown envelope positioned inside the arrangement of candles catches my attention. On the left-hand side of the room, next to another door, there is an inset fireplace. The embers glow a dull orange. A huge stockpile of wood and smaller kindling stands next to it, and there is a heavy looking poker leaning against its side. The right-hand side of the room is monopolised by a huge cooking stove, and pots and pans hang from a huge wooden beam that spans the entire length of the ceiling. Stone walls surround me once more, but they are illuminated with a soft orange glow. I still have no recollection of this place.

I slowly limp over to the table and inspect the envelope that rests against a small box. The name Benedict is written in the top left-hand corner in the most beautiful handwriting. I pick it up and trace my fingers over the gentle curves of the letters. The scribe is familiar to me, a sweeping font that I have seen somewhere before.

The voice of a woman emerges from behind me and softly utters "Benedict." I turn swiftly, but there is nobody there. That voice is also familiar. Suddenly, I feel sick. My stomach is churning and the same sense of foreboding sweeps over me. This woman, who is she to me? Why can't I remember anything?

As I draw the envelope close to my nostrils, the sweet scent begins to envelop me, and the sick feeling gives way to a cocktail of emotions: happiness, pain, love, and loss. But with no story behind them, I am left feeling disoriented. I close my eyes and suddenly I am somewhere else.

I can smell it, the dank woody smell of rotting leaves, and now I can hear the creak of the trees as they give to the wind. The sun filters through the canopy above, and the long grass sways in the cool breeze. I feel my lips on her warm neck, and I can taste her perfume; the mixture of flesh and scent is beginning to arouse me, and she knows it.

"Benedict, not here." She laughs, and her voice brings me to rapture.

It is a perfect moment. I know there is no other woman for me in the world. "Will you marry me?" I whisper into her ear.

And the vision fades. Only the scent remains.

I feel unhinged, as though I am not part of this world. My thoughts are monopolised with this woman, but who is she?

I hold the envelope out and study it once again. Part of me wants to rip it open—there must be some backstory in there, some clues as to who I am. But another part of me is scared to uncover the truth.

My fingers are visibly trembling as I slide them inside the envelope and draw the letter out:

Dearest Benedict.

You will always be the love of my life. I want you to know that.

Alas, this change that I see in you chills me to my bones. I do fear for my life now, especially after your last episode. Sometimes you look at me as though I am the most important thing in the world to you, other times you eye me like an enemy.

I cannot keep locking you in those chains. You need help, Benedict.

Tears fall as I write this, but I do not care to induce sadness from you. I have experienced more happiness with you than I ever thought I would in my entire lifetime.

My memories of the 'perfect you' are locked away in a vault, and I will draw upon them always.

Yours

Charlotte

xxx

I hold the envelope to my chest and will for more memories of her. But none come.

This episodic existence is unbearable. My life is made up of fragments that I cannot piece together. What is happening?

I focus hard to try and conjure up some more of the past. And some glimpses appear: holding hands with Charlotte on a country lane, chasing each other across the wet sand, the theatre, horse riding—and then another woman's face suddenly invades the vision. She has no eyes, and part of her cheek is missing. Her long brown hair is matted into the wound, and her head has been roughly detached from her body.

I shake my head to try and dislodge the image, but she won't go away. Why do I see this?

"It's okay, Benedict. It doesn't matter how hard it gets. I could never leave you, my darling." That voice again.

She appears, sitting in the large oak chair opposite me, her beauty amplified by the soft glow of the candles. We raise our wine glasses and toast our future. I push the chair away and dance my way around the table, and she laughs, a hearty laugh for someone so petite. Her long brown curls dance, too, as she throws her own chair behind and struts to the middle with arms outstretched. Her skin is like porcelain, and her eyes so green they remind me of spring—when nature comes alive. I twirl her, and the brown dress comes alive, too, and our shadows dance larger than life on the stone wall. A smile forms across my face, accompanied by a stinging pain on my right cheek. And with that, the memory is gone and I am standing next to the table, arms and hands outstretched, envelope in one and on the other my fingers arch towards my lonely shadow on the far wall.

What went wrong?

I place the envelope back against the small box and another image of Charlotte immediately invades my head. She is smiling, her eyes moist with tears as I remove the ring from the box and ask for her hand in marriage. And just as quickly, she is gone.

These fleeting memories are all I have, but they invoke in me great feelings of love, passion, and loss. These glimpses of happiness feel cruel to me right now.

As I hobble across to the wooden door near the fireplace—possibly a portal for more pieces of history— the sweet perfume scent begins to fade. My nostrils are beginning to fill with a different and less pleasant odour, one that is beginning to lay at the back of my throat. There is something unpleasant behind this door. I know it.

I reach for the handle, and the door clicks without resistance. I pause for a second and even contemplate closing it again—but I need all the pieces.

As it swings open, I immediately see a foot dangling a few yards in front of me at eye level. The other foot is missing; nothing but exposed bone and blood. A puddle of congealed darkness has collected on the stone underneath along with a gathering of large flies. My heart rate intensifies and is accompanied by a sudden constriction in my chest. I can't get any air in. The feeling of falling washes over me and, with nothing to cling to, I collapse on the floor and drop the candle. The flame dies immediately, and I am in darkness again with only the company of the swinging corpse and the flies. The victim's head is angled towards me, black holes where the eyes should be, tears of crimson all the way down to the chin. Both arms are completely missing from the shoulders, and the brittle long brown hair drapes across her cheeks and over the open sockets.

My first thought is that it isn't Charlotte.

I kick my legs and again wince in pain as I try and shuffle away to put some distance between us. The gentle sway of the body gives it some animation, and I half expect it to speak. Only a few feet from my right hand I see a stone table and a rusty jagged saw covered in familiar crimson stains resting against it. Atop the table, I can make out the wooden handle of some other tool that no doubt played a part in this brutality. The makeshift winch is on the other side of the wall, chains twisting around metal and leading up to the beam from where her body hangs. Solid wooden ladders stand next to it, a trail of blood leading down each rung.

What is this place?

My stomach begins to churn at the horror my eyes are feeding it and, unable to bear it any longer, I jump up and rush back into the main dining area. Adrenaline alleviates some of the pain in my leg, but it still drags behind me awkwardly. When I reach the edge of the table, I grab it and begin to dry heave.

What the hell? Did I do this?

Sitting down on one of the wooden chairs, I try and collect my thoughts, but my mind is blank—too many missing pieces. My hands are shaking vigorously, and my right knee is bouncing up and down anxiously.

It suddenly feels ten degrees colder in here. My blood feels like icy water.

I walk over to the fire and, as I bend down to grab the poker, something catches my eye amongst the pile of glowing embers. Displacing some of the burnt wood and ashes, I uncover what look to be fragments of charred bone. I recoil initially, but then urgently start rifling through the other embers only to find more remains. One of the bones resembles a humorous.

How do I know that?

I reel back and begin to convulse, and this time solid pieces of chewed meat project onto the floor. It is all too much. I want to believe that I am not responsible, that this is someone else's doing. But something in those stranger's eyes staring back in that shard of glass made my skin crawl.

Stumbling across to the table, I try and take some deep breaths. I am lost in a world of confusion, and the anger continues to rise. As my fist slams against the wooden table, the candles jump, and my hand sends a bolt of pain up my arm that does nothing to dilute my rage.

"What is happening to me?" I scream. But the question only echoes back.

I begin to cry. I feel so helplessly alone.

I need to get her back, to find her and apologise for whatever I have done. I need to know what is going on.

After picking the rest of the bones from the fire, I grab an old rag from near the stove and wrap them inside. In need of some comforting warmth, I place fresh wood on the fire and stoke it until the chill in the room begins to subside.

As I open the front door, the fresh breeze is well received, and there, sitting on the stone bench next to the path, is the love of my life. She turns to me. "What have you got there, Benedict?"

But before I can answer, she is gone.

Another memory: Charlotte kneeling in front of me, gently placing the shackles around my wrist. She locks them and kisses me on the forehead before walking to the iron door but before fully closing it, she turns, and I know what she is going to say.

"Why does this happen, Benedict?"

I look at her and can see a combination of fear and pity in her eyes.

"I don't know. Please leave now," I say.

And now I am looking at the empty bench again, a handful of human bones in my arms. I carry them down the side of the house towards the back. I have no idea why, but it just feels right, familiar. When I see the large hole in the centre of my yard, I know it immediately to be a makeshift grave, big enough for a human body. A mound of earth sits next to it, ready to fill some poor victim's mouth. A shovel rests against the side of the stone house.

I am trying to feel something—shock, horror, disgust—but nothing registers. I am numb. The feeling of nausea is gone and being replaced with something else. I am not sure what, but I am beginning to feel different.

Another memory fills my head: full moon, no breeze, and I stand in the hole throwing earth behind me frantically. I am smiling, but it's an unnatural curvature of the lips that displays too many teeth. It is me, but it isn't. Something has possessed this version, this murderer.

The memory fades.

I can no longer convince myself that these wrongdoings do not fall at my hands. These visions or memories or whatever they are, they are too vivid.

I remember finding the letter. The ink had not dried. I recall the feeling of loneliness and helplessness, but also the rage at being abandoned.

Without her, I know that I will kill again.

It might not be too late.

Perhaps I can win her back. We can make a fresh start, fix whatever went wrong. *The bitch will come back.* The thought drifts into my head, and I shake it away.

It is already getting dark, and something is beginning to stir inside me, a combination of dread and excitement at the unpredictability of night. I throw the bones in the hole and rush back inside.

The winch creaks and rattles as I rotate the handle and lower the body down. Grimacing, I reach for the dry hair and drag the woman's body across the stone floor and outside to the rear of the house where I ease her mutilated corpse into the large open pit. I strip off my clothes and toss them on top of her.

As I stand naked looking into her eyeless eyes, the words come. "I love you, Charlotte. Please come back to me."

And she does.

I take the hand of my darling, and we dance around the grave edge, twisting and twirling for minutes. Her laughter is bliss to me and, once again, I want this moment with her to last forever. She looks at me and smiles, my reflection entrapped in the greens of her eyes. But the smile quickly fades as she turns to look at the lady in the grave. "Who's that?"

"That is nobody, Charlotte."

I grab the shovel and bring it down on the woman's head. "See," I say. And again. The impact vibrates up my arm as the shovel collides with the bone. And again. The edge of it sinks into her neck this time, and I wrestle it free and continue to bring it down and slice through her skin.

Soon the face is half gone.

I continue to pound her relentlessly with the makeshift weapon, and now the vision I had before doesn't seem so out of character. I stop, breathing laboured and arms aching from this episode of brutality.

What kind of monster am I?

When I turn around, Charlotte is gone.

"Why do you keep leaving?" I scream.

I am drifting in and out of this deranged state, but there is undoubtedly a transformation taking place. I am starting to feel powerful again and in control. Beating my chest, I howl loudly into the dusky night. I am coming alive—this is my calling.

I will make her come back.

My arms feel like lead and the palm of my hand is throbbing, but I get to work and start placing the earth back over her degraded body. I flatten it out as neatly as possible as the last few shovels go on, but the surrounding soil is just as uneven, and I have already lost interest and start on a new grave for the inevitable next victim.

Inside, I throw some wood on the fire and begin to coax a flame. The warmth is well received. Another memory: Charlotte and I making love in front of this fire, our bodies glistening with each other's sweat, as though we were melting into one. And then it fades, but the pain remains. I know that I love this woman.

How could she leave when I needed her most?

Memories and emotions are beginning to awaken, and I am slowly rebuilding my past. Charlotte is the key. I remember trying to explain it to her once. I wanted to be able to rationalise it in a way that would make sense but couldn't. When the sun goes down, I begin to feel different. Charged is the word I would use. It is a combination of excitement, arousal, and fury that builds, and I recall trying to convince her that it was under control.

But recently, the thoughts have grown darker. I am feeling more unpredictable, volatile, and dangerous.

There is no longer a need to keep it in, no need for chains—not since she left. When she comes back, she will need to learn to accept me for who I am. And she will come back.

My anger rises with the flames. I know who I am now.

Evil has always been with me, a malignancy living inside my head. For years it has fed my thoughts, my visions, and provided compulsions so dark and twisted—and there are times that I have come dangerously close to acting them out. And then I met Charlotte and, somehow, she neutralised them, gave me something to believe in outside of the voices. I felt true love for the first time, and she was beginning to unlock emotions and feelings I thought I was incapable of feeling. But she took them away with her, and I have only dark thoughts again—nothing to counterbalance. All of this is her fault.

"My name is Benedict," I say out loud. "Benedict."

After scrubbing the bloodstains from the floor and washing the bowl and cup that were left near the door, I sniff the letter from my dearest once again before dressing, wrapping up in my thickest jacket, and leaving the house.

Tomorrow I will set off early to find Charlotte. Tonight will be my last indulgence.

I have no idea where I am going initially, but, once again, it just feels right. The path becomes familiar the more I walk, and before long I am at the dockyards, and the first few whores come into sight.

Hiding behind a tree, I make a hissing sound to get the nearest one's attention. She looks up, catches my gaze, and smiles. She is no doubt used to this type of exchange and begins to walk over. To my delight, she has long brown curly hair—just like my Charlotte. It is too dark to see the colour of her eyes.

I see some slight surprise register across her face when I request her services. Charlotte was always telling me how handsome I am, and the whore even has the nerve to ask me why I can't find a good wholesome girl. I surprise myself by telling her that I did once, but she left.

I offer her a good sum of money to come to the house, and she accepts. I am firm in telling her no conversation is required, and we walk home in silence.

As we open the front door of the house, the warm orange glow greets us, and the fire is still throwing out some heat.

"This is nice," she says, breaking the forced silence.

I haven't even asked her name and have no intention of doing so.

"Hungry?" I ask. "I know I am."

She looks at me and smiles. "I am actually. What is your name?"

Her eyes are brown.

"Benedict," I reply. "I am Benedict."

"Let me take that for you," I say, removing her jacket.

"It's Anna," she shouts as I carry it through to the room where the day began.

The adrenaline kicks in as soon as I see the chains, and I steady myself against the wall. I take a breath and close my eyes. *Control, Benedict. Savour the moment.* But my enjoyment is harshly interrupted as the scene plays out in my head.

I am bent down on the floor holding the shackles out towards her. I see myself shaking. My face is turning red. I am telling Charlotte to hurry up.

"I don't want to do this anymore, B," she says as she fumbles for them and tries to clasp them around my wrist. "I'm scared of you," she mumbles.

My face is twisted in an unflattering way. The handsomeness has gone, and I am looking at her as though it is taking all my effort not to reach out and rip her heart out. I can see murder in my eyes.

"You need to leave now, Charlotte! Get out!"

"B! You're scaring me!"

I see myself rush to the mirror and begin to inspect the reflection as though I am suddenly going to sprout hairs and fangs. "Go," I scream. And then I begin throwing my head against the glass. The accompanying scream from Charlotte is far from silent, and she stands frozen to the spot as my head continues to pound into the mirror. Eventually, I stop and turn to her. My eyes are blank, but an uneven snarl broadcasts my intent.

She tries to run, but I quickly pick up one of the shards and grab her by the chin, twisting her body around to face me.

"Don't do it," I scream at myself.

"Benedict, please," the plea for mercy leaves her lips.

As I hover the glass over her head, I am growling and biting at the air, saliva spraying everywhere, and I let out a howl that sounds inhuman.

But I remember that I couldn't do it. How could I? She is my soul mate. It was the green of her eyes; they took me back to the woods and the cocktail of damp leaves and perfume and the softness of the ground beneath. I remember so intensely fighting the urge to bring that glass down into her eye, shaking violently against the instinct to cut and slice.

I watch myself bring the glass down deep into my thigh, and the echo from the pain runs up my leg. The monster falls to the ground with a subsequent guttural howl. And she runs.

I open my eyes, and I am back, the shard of glass shaking in front of me. I don't even remember picking it up. Blood spills down its edge from the reopened wound, leaking fresh crimson onto the whore's jacket on the ground.

I am ravenous, more than I ever remember.

Her smile fades, and she starts to scream as I rush at her. She puts her hands in front, but I easily push them aside and ram the glass into her eye socket. Her hands are flailing as I lift the weapon and bring it down into the other eye. Her fingernails catch the wound on the side of my face, and it opens again, but adrenaline is flowing and there is no pain. She continues to reach out futilely, but she surely knows her time is done.

I run the glass across her throat and feel the blood as it sprays my face. She is gurgling now; small bubbles are forming around her neck. Her legs kick wildly and in vain, the final movements before death. I hold her hand as she passes. It's the least I can do.

The knife slides against bone as I gently prise out one of the eyes. I study it closely: pretty but not close to being as beautiful as Charlotte's. It makes a popping sound between my teeth, bursting open, and provides a fresh and meaty taste. I recall the slightly crunchy centre from last time.

As the rest of it slips down my throat, I grab her by the hair and drag her body through to my workshop. This room that initially provided fear and repulsion now feels familiar and comforting to me.

My home. My tools. And this is what I do.

I circle the chain around her neck and begin to winch her up. But I am hungry and impatient and carve some of the soft flesh from her thigh before hoisting her to full height. Standing underneath, I arch my head and catch some of the fresh blood on my tongue as it rains downs.

I am Benedict.

Excitedly I rush through to the kitchen and, after taking the sharpest knife from the drawer, I begin to slice and dice the meat before placing it into the iron skillet. My mouth begins to water as I hold the meat over the fire. It cooks slowly, but that is fine with me. My thoughts turn back to Charlotte.

"This is your fault," I whisper.

Even as a child, I remember the dark thoughts, the prickling of the hairs on the back of my neck as I was dragged into church every Sunday morning. Mother died before I knew her, and Father thought going to church would keep us close to her. I hated it.

I knew I wasn't normal, but I learned to fake it, to appear human, blend in. My father always knew. The way he looked at me gave it away. My secret died with him, and I no longer had anyone to pretend to— until I met Charlotte.

I pick out the chunks of meat that look ready and enjoy the perfect moistness in my mouth. After the rest of it cooks, I scrape into a bowl and then place it on the tray along with a cup of water next to my chamber door. First thing in the morning I will eat, and then set off to find my Charlotte.

The beast inside is calming now and it is nearly time to rest. But before I retire to my chamber, I walk over to the table, grab the envelope and run it under my nose once again. The scent is fading—all I have of her is nearly gone.

My eyes fall on the small blue box again and I find myself staring at it for a while. A familiar uneasiness begins to wash over me. Curiously, I pick it up and slowly remove the lid. As my eyes fall on the contents inside, something inside me breaks, and I fall to the floor, clinging the box to my chest.

"No, no, no, no! That can't be." I mutter.

The eyes no longer shine with life. The lush green has already started to fade, along with any chance of salvation.

The grief washes over me, and I begin to bawl like a child, an accompanying pain surges across my chest.

"What have I done?" I scream.

The ink was still dry.

She should have put the chains on when she had the chance.

Rocking back and forth, I am once again feeling lost. My mind is broken, censoring pieces of the past but then cruelly feeding me memories of this maniac that lives inside me.

"I'm sorry, Charlotte, but you belong here with me. I couldn't let you go."

I place the eyes back into the box and put the envelope back in place. This little shrine is all I have left of my beloved.

"Goodnight, my love," I whisper before making my way back to the chamber.

I am a monster with a broken heart, and I need to be caught.

The beast has well and truly left, and I feel weak now, exhausted. The blankets offer little comfort, but my eyes are already becoming heavy. The fog is returning.

***

The smell is familiar, but not comforting.

Wing and a Prayer

A two-lane blacktop road snaked up into the distance, disappearing into some trees. It also invited them down toward some lumpy hills and disappeared there, as well. What sounded like a two-stroke chainsaw could be heard in the distance.

Tom stared down at his phone, willing bars into existence, but not even one appeared, and the battery was nearly dead anyway. Everyone else's phone had been stolen the last time they stepped out of the vehicle to get snacks and directions.

Kicking the tyre and throwing his empty can onto the grass verge, Greg suggested—at the top of his lungs—that Tom was a fucking moron.

Tom didn't rise to the bait. Stopping at a fuel station that looked like it had been resurrected from a '70s horror movie didn't appeal, not when someone had already smashed the car window at the last stop and taken their phones and most of their cash—the only evidence left behind: a couple of black feathers on the back seat. Besides, he was sure they would last out until the next filling station, hopefully somewhere more conventional. But he'd never driven his Dad's car before and didn't realise just how thirsty the El Dorado was.

The invitation gave nothing away, the name Nevar and vague directions sketched in thick black ink. This strange summons left at both Holly and Greg's door—and a truckload of curiosity—was why they were now stuck in the middle of god knows where. There was certainly something odd about the place; he felt it a few miles back when the hairs on the back of his neck began to prickle. Shortly after that, he thought he saw something in the woods, and ever since he'd had a feeling they were being watched.

The wooded areas on either side of the road seemed to be getting denser. And the further they drove, the more Tom began to note the conspicuous absence of signposts, as though the place wasn't keen on newcomers. Only the birds seemed to treat the location as home. Two hundred yards back, they had seen quite a spectacle: an almost symmetrical circle of crows surrounding the carcass of one of their own. Tom had slowed down considerably, as a mark of respect, much to the disgust of Greg.

It was Holly who'd suggested the road trip as a way of celebrating their graduation. She'd also said that it would help take Tom's mind off his father dying. But last week Tom had seen her with her tongue down some guy's throat, so he wasn't entirely sure his best interests were her priority.

Even before he knew Greg was coming, Tom hadn't been keen. Disregarding the fact that he'd once dated Holly, he hated creepy Greg with a passion. Silver spoon type, privileged. Arsehole.

Vanessa seemed nice enough. Guarded, but pleasant. It could have been his imagination, and it sounded corny, but he sensed something between them as soon as they met. It wasn't physical as such, rather a compulsion to be around her, as though it was the natural order of things. She had a nice face, not what his mates would call a looker, so to speak, but pretty in an old-fashioned sense. He wanted to know everything about her.

Vanessa stepped out of the car. The smell of the damp leaves and grass blew away some of the staleness of the El Dorado. The place reminded her of home and prompted a sharp pang of nostalgia and loneliness as she observed the rolling hills and lush greens. She missed home. But she couldn't stay after what happened. She knew it was the loneliness that had led her to Greg, but it was becoming apparent very quickly that agreeing to date him had made a big mistake.

As if on cue, Greg released a loud sigh and thumped his fist on the hood of the car in another unnecessary show of machismo.

"Hey, Greg. Not on the car, please," Tom shouted.

"It will be your head next, Tommy." He smirked. "Where have you brought us, for Christ's sake?"

Tom felt his anger rising. It wasn't just Greg's jock-type looks that made him sick to the stomach—blue eyes, slicked-back blond hair, and six-pack—but his attitude was off the charts.

Holly was out next. "Yes, Tom. Where the fuck are we?" she said, one arm on her hip, her nose wrinkled.

Oh, don't you start.

"Breathe in, Holly. Smell the air. It's delicious," Tom said.

"It smells like cow shit," she replied.

"You two are the reason we are here. Don't blame me for this." Tom sighed and watched Greg retrieve the sunglasses from his shirt pocket even though there was no sign of the sun.

Tom hated it when Holly put on this routine. She was undoubtedly attractive in the conventional sense, with her long bleached-blonde hair, slim figure, and whitened teeth. But he thought how exhausting it must be to play the bitch. On a shallow level, he'd enjoyed the initial kudos from his mates, but glimpses of the real Holly were so few and far between that it started to wear thin on him. Not to mention the numerous infidelities—the ones he saw and the ones that got reported back. When the timing is right, he would end it—that's what he kept telling himself, anyway.

The four of them stood in a line looking at the two roads ahead until Greg took a coin from his pocket and flipped it high in the air. They watched as it merged into the dull sky and finally began its descent, hitting Holly square on the bridge of her nose before landing on the tarmac and rolling over to tails.

Caw!

The loud cry exploded behind them.

"Jesus," Holly shouted and followed up with a nervous giggle. She was visibly shaken.

The crow looked at each of them individually with its head slightly cocked, its plumage black and glossy and appearing even more sinister against the black sheen of the El Dorado. The bird glanced them over one more time and, apparently unimpressed, flew off towards the forest.

"I vote to follow the crow," Tom said.

"No way. Only one crow is bad luck," Holly replied. "I thought everyone knew that."

Tom started walking in the direction that the crow flew. Vanessa followed. She had already decided to follow the bird, but if it meant getting away from the walking talking cardboard cut-out called Greg, that would be a bonus. She already knew she liked Tom. He was funny and exponentially smarter than most college grads. Not someone she'd call handsome, but with a nice face that came alive when he smiled. His thick black hair and matching eyebrows made his pale skin look even more pallid. But there was something about him, something that made her feel safe, and that was a major achievement.

Holly was always right, even when she was wrong, and Greg had bet on tails and there was no arguing with that. So the group split into two. Tom and Vanessa would follow their new friend up to the forest, and Greg and Holly would head down towards the hills. At the first sign of civilisation, they would find a phone and make the call for Nevar to retrieve them.

***

For some time, Tom and Vanessa walked in comfortable silence. The woods seemed to be getting denser, and there was a stronger smell, too: a cocktail of damp leaves and pine that caught Tom completely off guard. It took him back the days of hiking and climbing with his father back home, something they used to do a lot. But cancer fucked that up. He wished his father had been there to see him graduate. He would have been so proud. As far as the El Dorado went, though, he would have given him stick about running out of gas, and he had to smile at that.

"What's on your mind, stranger?" Vanessa asked.

"Oh, nothing really."

But she had one eyebrow up and he knew he wasn't getting away that easily.

"My father. I'm not sure if Holly told you, but he passed away recently."

"No, she didn't. We don't really have deep and meaningful conversations. Favourite band, movie star, alcohol, that's as far as it goes really. I'm sorry to hear about your father."

"I've been okay for the last couple of weeks, but I've struggled today. I think it was the El Dorado, to be honest. It's the first time I've driven it. And for that dickhead Greg to put his feet on the dash and smash the—sorry, I—I wasn't thinking. How stupid—"

"Whoa, slow down, cowboy," Vanessa interjected. "Greg is a douche. A fleeting mistake in my life. Let me make that clear right now."

"You really like him, then?" Tom smiled. "So what's the deal? We know so little about you."

"There isn't much to say."

"Okay. No. If I'm not allowed to get away with that kind of bullshit, you don't get a pass, either."

"Look, Tom. I'm not being funny, but I really don't want to go there today. Please." she replied with half a smile.

"Sorry, I didn't mean to pry. Well, I did, but you know what I mean."

She laughed. "I do. And I have a strange feeling that I'll tell you one day. Just not today."

They carried on walking in silence for a few minutes.

And then they noticed the birds. Dozens of hyperactive crows had started lining the trees either side of them for as far as they could see, and it made for a sinister sight. Tom was starting to feel as though they were the drawcard.

They were close to the peak of the hill now, and the chainsaw was getting unmistakably louder and, with it, the excitement level of the crows in the tree. They were dancing from side to side and swinging their beaks around to the raucous soundtrack. Vanessa and Tom looked at each other, but neither of them attempted an explanation.

Tom retrieved the invitation from his jeans pocket only to find the head of a large black crow was all that remained. He showed the piece of card to Vanessa.

"I had a strange feeling about this place, Tom. A while back. As though we really should not be here."

"Yeah, me too, Vee."

He didn't know why he called her that. It just sort of slipped out.

She expected to feel a sharper reaction: a knot in her stomach or instant palpitations. The bastard that ruined her was the last person to call her that. In a different time and place. A town that she could never return to. But there was no such reaction.

As they finally reached the peak of the hill, the chainsaw stopped abruptly, as did the movement of the crows. An eerie silence fell. Vanessa looked across at Tom. Almost immediately, the silence was shattered by an almighty piercing and bone-rattling caw. She felt the hairs on the back of her neck rise, and her heart began to thump. Soon the dull sky got duller as huge clouds of crows swept towards them — from above, from the trees, and the other side of the peak — coming together to form a large black wall that moved towards them at tremendous speed, twisting and turning with a menacing ferocity.

"Dive," Tom shouted as he threw himself on the ground.

Vanessa followed just in time and the crows swept over their heads by inches. Tom's elbow smacked against the ground, and he winced but could not tear his eyes away from the dark formation. He glanced to his left and saw Vanessa with her hands around the back of her head lying face down on the ground.

For a moment the crows circled above, and Tom steadied himself for another attack, but instead, they quickly dispersed as a large man dressed up as a crow stepped out the woods with a chainsaw in hand. He bowed.

"Greetings. My name is Nevar. It's good to meet you," he said, slowly straightening. A large crow flew down from one of the trees and perched on his shoulder.

Perfectly normal, Tom thought. He looked over at Vanessa, who was still face down in the ground with her eyes screwed tightly shut.

***

"How are things going with Vanessa?" Holly asked.

"Fine. She'll do for now. Why, are you jealous?"

"Not likely. Been there, done that, got the shitty T-shirt, thanks."

The sound of the chainsaw was fading and, with it, Holly's vision of a psychopath jumping out and slashing their heads off with it. The place gave her the creeps, and she was beginning to wish that she hadn't pushed Tom into making the drive out. She hated how stubborn he was sometimes, but on this occasion, she realised she should have listened.

Being alone with Greg in the middle of nowhere was bringing back some of the uneasy feelings and dark memories. Rarely sober, often high on anything she could get her hands on—she wished she could wipe away that period of her life. Even now, she still wasn't right and knew she probably never would be. Tom once told her she needed more self-worth. The little shit. Easy to say for someone that lives in a bubble.

"Do you ever think about us?" Greg asked.

"No, I don't. Back then, I was a different person."

"Yeah, I know. It was great. Why are you with that square Tom anyway? Anyone can see he's not your type."

"He's a nice guy. Steady."

"You mean boring," Greg snapped and followed his words with a surly laugh.

In hindsight, she wished she had gone with Tom—and all because of that stupid crow.

Holly stopped, raising her arm towards a black shape about two hundred yards away on the side of the road. They set off in a slow jog but soon scaled back to a walk when the object became clearer. Neither of them said anything as they stared at the person dressed like a crow sitting on the edge of the road, its head buried beneath makeshift wings. It was the first of many that lined the roads for as far as they could see.

Greg finally strutted over to the mysterious figure. "I'm hoping you can help us. We're a bit lost."

As soon as he got close, the crow-person jumped up and gave a single hostile caw before flapping its wings and commencing to run around in tiny circles. Greg turned to look at Holly and frowned. Seizing the opportunity, the crow-person pulled a needle from its feathers, swooped in, and jabbed it hard into Greg's neck. His eyes instantly rolled back and he collapsed into the crow-person's wings. Holly tried to scream, but the sight of so many crow-people flapping their wings and bounding towards her—all squawking wildly—prevented her from anything but a whimper. She felt the needle plunge into her arm—and she thought she heard herself give a little caw.

**

Vanessa was still cleaning herself off when Nevar put the chainsaw down and began to walk over. He extended a hand from the feathery arm and she offered hers in return and gave him a firm handshake. The bird left his shoulder but continued to watch from the branch of a nearby tree.

Tom was slower in raising his hand. "That was … intense."

"Welcome to our home," Nevar said. "Your friends are being looked after. Come."

Vanessa wanted to ask how he could possibly know about their friends and especially their wellbeing. But she was talking to a man in a crow's costume and decided it might be prudent to leave her questions for later.

The crow man cawed gently and within seconds more crow-people appeared from behind the large trees. Before long, a giant feathery army was working in unison piling chopped wood onto the back of a rickety cart.

Nevar apologised for the vague directions, but explained, "We never stay in one place for long; we are a very private flock. Thus the temporary ink. Come, let's walk."

Tom noted the use of the word flock and thought the day was getting weirder by the minute.

"It's hard for outsiders to relate, but we are a very spiritual folk, beyond the realms of what you could possibly comprehend. And please do not take that personally. Our flock's ethos is based on hundreds of years of tradition and belief. What you and your friends might refer to as folklore I suppose." He smiled a warm but serious smile.

Vanessa caught Tom by surprise by saying, "I've never come across anything like this before—Nevar, was it? What's the deal with the crows?"

"My new friends, let me give you the short version. We have been celebrating the crow for hundreds of years. The crow is a messenger between the world of the living and the world of the dead. In layman's terms, when people cannot peacefully pass on to their new life, their spirit crow seeks us out and we do what we can to help them pass over."

Nevar looked from the ground to Vanessa and she nodded calmly. Personally, Tom was starting to feel incredibly nervous and wasn't sure he could duplicate such composure.

Nevar continued, "Then there are the evil souls, the ones that don't deserve to pass from this world. Their spirits are imprisoned in the crow until death takes it—their penance for the evil acts they committed."

Vanessa glanced at Tom. He shrugged.

"You probably think I'm crazy," Nevar said. "Look, we're having a huge ceremony to celebrate tonight, and we would be honoured to have you as our guests. I won't take no for an answer."

His demeanour turned jovial and his face lit up with excitement. He shook his feathers and cawed in appreciation. Then, as though welcoming them into the fold, he swept his wing in a broad gesture of pride and delight to unveil his home: a large clearing full of wooden shacks and improvised shelters made from branches. Adults and children dressed in crow ensembles sat around a large fire singing and dancing, playing tag and climbing trees.

**

Holly began to stir. She knew it wasn't a dream as she could still feel where the needle entered her arm. Her eyes opened slowly, squinting as the sunshine filtered through the hut. She tried to scream, but there was tape across her mouth. Still blurry, she tried to get up but found her arms and legs bound to the bed with twine. There was a crow perched on the end of the bed, and she felt as though it was staring into her soul. It gave a single caw and flew off. The crow-person leaned over her and whispered the name Jessica into her ear, and she immediately began to sob. She regretted the day she'd checked Greg's phone. None of it would have happened. She'd just wanted to teach the girl a lesson, let everyone know that nobody messed with Holly Webster.

**

Greg was throwing himself around, trying to spit the gag out. He had woken up in a wooden shack with his legs and hands tied. It was empty apart from the crow perched on the end of the bed. The large bird hopped on his feet and walked the full length of his body to his head before giving him a swift and sharp poke in the eye with its beak and then flying out the door. One of the crow minions walked in and uttered the name Jessica, and he stopped struggling immediately.

As soon as the gag was removed, Greg started screaming, "That wasn't me. It was that bitch Holly. She's the one you want!"

The crow-person put the gag back in his mouth, cawed once, and left.

"Hey, let me out of here, bird-face," he screamed.

Seconds later, two more crow-people replaced the first. Greg felt some of the twines loosen as he started throwing himself around, but the needle was plunged once more into his neck and his struggling ceased.

**

"My new friends, it has been great talking to you, but, alas, I need to get ready for tonight's proceedings," Nevar proclaimed. "Make sure they get whatever they want," he said to two of his flock before turning back, giving a final bow, and walking off in the direction of the huts.

They were led through to a makeshift arena with an abundance of beautiful solid wood tables. Barrels of wine were being rolled into the area, all sporting large crows carved into their sides. Food was being delivered from all directions: huge dead animals on spits and endless platters of potatoes and vegetables. It was an impressive sight, and there was an obvious excitement as the flock prepared for the evening. Tom and Vanessa felt it, too. The foreboding feeling Tom had was beginning to dissipate. Nevar was an odd but interesting chap, but he felt no threat. Besides, he was starting to look forward to what the night might have in store for him and Vanessa. Greg and Holly could look after themselves.

Nevar arrived at the end of the clearing and entered the nearest shack. He greeted the existing guard with a caw and moved to Holly's side. Holding his phone to her mouth, he ripped off the tape and asked her to admit her part in Jessica's death. She sobbed her confession. Nevar thanked her and told her she would be dead by midnight.

***

Greg woke up to the stare of another bird person and uttered a muffled profanity before trying to wrestle himself free. Nevar clicked his fingers, and the crow came swooping through the window, landing on Greg's forehead. It flapped its wings and gave a gentle caw before steadying itself and hovering its beak just a couple of inches away from his eye. Greg started to swing his head from left to right, but the bird jumped and shuffled in perfect time. Nevar held out the phone and told him to confess or the next time he clicked his fingers, the crow would be feeding on his eye. He started to protest, but as soon as Nevar put his fingers together, Greg squawked as though his life depended on it. He was told that it didn't and that he was dead as soon as he touched Jessica.

***

She'd been found by her mum, wrists open and bath overflowing. No note but Facebook open on her laptop, naked photos of her plastered across the screen in various poses with horrendous comments posted: slut, bitch, whore. She'd been a virgin until she met Greg.

***

Three crow-people came in, one of them carrying a small sack with two eyeholes. When Holly refused to take it, they hit her twice in the face. She heard her nose snap. Reluctantly, she grabbed the sack, but when they handed over the white robe and she caught sight of her own crimson blood splashing onto the stark white material, she ran.

***

Nevar cawed to some of his disciples and asked them to fetch a blanket and wine for his two guests. For a moment, Tom thought he saw a naked woman running out of one of the shacks and into the dense woodland. He shrugged and began to fill his plate with food.

The evening was drawing in and the anticipation was continuing to build. Vanessa looked at Tom. He smiled, and she thought the day was turning out fine. She didn't know what was happening between them, but it couldn't be ignored. He was a good man—far too good for Holly. After knowing her for only a few weeks, she already knew about two other men she'd kissed. According to Holly, "only sex is cheating"; anything else was just having fun. But that wasn't how Vanessa felt. And she was pretty sure that Tom would concur. Anyway, Holly wasn't there, and the night was young.

***

Holly was setting quite a pace. For a city girl, she was fast on her feet. Their feathers seemed to be slowing her pursuers down as they ran against the wind. She had the fleeting thought that it was certainly a scene—her naked female form being chased relentlessly by two people dressed up as crows. In any other circumstance, she thought it would have been farcical, but here she was—she assumed—running for her life. The real crow was flying above her, watching her every move. It sounded its call and was soon accompanied by a dozen others. They descended, maintaining their formation, and then launched their assault. Holly thrashed erratically at the crows. Some bore the brunt of her swipes but soon re-joined the fight. They were everywhere—and she couldn't see more than a yard in front. Eventually, she started flying, too, as she caught her right foot on a protruding root. She came crashing down into the ground, knocking herself out on the base of a knotty tree. The crows circled her in a manner reminiscent of the scene the four had witnessed earlier—except she was the one being mourned.

***

Nevar knelt in his shack in front of the makeshift shrine, a single photograph of his daughter Jessica the only decoration.

A single crow had been perched on her grave when he last visited; stubbornly, it did not fly off, even when he advanced. It had a reason to be there, he allowed, and so they had paid their respects together. The day after the graveside meeting, a crow had perched itself on the fence outside the kitchen window of the shack he rented. He swore it was the same crow that had perched on his daughter's grave. The bird came back every day for a month, and he soon became fascinated with it. He began to read everything he could about the species and was amazed by the intelligence of the bird. He studied its behaviour, and the symbolism and history behind it—so many reports of its connection to the afterlife and destiny. And then he came across the folklore and reported sightings of the mysterious crow-people.

One day he got in the car and followed the crow.

For two years, he had immersed himself in the tradition of the crow-people, sacrificing everything for the night ahead, pledging loyalty, and rising through the ranks. He was recognised and respected by the community. The crow ensemble made him feel powerful and spiritual—even virtuous.

And tonight, retribution would finally be his.

***

There was a drum roll and everyone went silent. Little crow children entered the arena and the crowd cheered. There was an energetic display of juggling and acrobatics and then a well-choreographed dance that someone told them was called The Flight of the Crow. The children took bows to enormous applause.

Nevar watched from the side and gestured for them to get on with the next act.

Some of the crow-people came out carrying a large steaming vat of liquid and trays of what appeared to be black feathers. Another formation wheeled out two huge wooden structures resembling gallows, made from the wood Nevar had chopped down earlier.

Tom quickly grabbed the edge of the table to steady himself and set his wine glass down. He eased back into the chair and hoped he wouldn't fall asleep. The wine had gone straight to his head, and his vision was becoming blurry.

The drum roll started again and two people dressed in robes were ushered into the arena. Their hands were tied at the front and they wore what looked like burlap sacks over their heads. Tom gave a thumbs-up to Vanessa before realising she was already face down on the table.

"Hey, Vee," he shouted.

She turned her head to face him, smiled, and closed her eyes.

Huge torches were lit and orange flames soon illuminated the arena. Two of the crow-people dipped their brushes into the viscous black liquid and started to paint the two robed people from head to toe. Tom thought he could hear screaming but couldn't be sure over the noise of the crowd. Some of the other crow-people started dancing around and throwing feathers at the robed people. Tom thought it looked like black confetti at some sinister wedding ceremony.

Fireworks started to light up the sky. Some of the crow-people entered the arena carrying a red carpet and laid it in front of a makeshift entrance. Catherine wheels were lit either side and then out came Nevar holding a microphone and looking as though he was about to start a sermon. Instead, he told his followers to "Lead the sinners to the stairs." The robed people were led up the steps onto a platform and ropes were put around their necks. Nevar counted down from three and on zero they were pushed off and fell what Tom estimated to be fifteen feet before their necks cocked and their bodies slowly and lifelessly began to sway like silent wind chimes.

The crowd went wild, dancing and squawking wildly.

Tom shouted across to a member of the audience how realistic it all looked, and they turned, winked, and continued their applause. Within seconds, blankets of crows swooped in from all directions and engulfed the swinging corpses.

Swaying from side to side, Tom was rapidly losing consciousness. His vision was one moment clear and the next a slow-motion blur of orange and black.

Just before he passed out, he saw the feathery predators grab the sacks with their claws and hoist them into the air, revealing his travelling companions' eyeless faces.

***

Vanessa was the first to wake and gave Tom a gentle nudge, and then a sharper one. He awoke with a start, putting a hand to his head to nurse the immediate pain. The wine was drugged, he decided. It must have been. And the last image of the evening suddenly flashed into his head and set his heart racing.

"Tom, where are we?" Vanessa asked.

The pounding in his heard was becoming even more violent, and he closed his eyes tightly as a wave of dizziness washed over him. When he opened them again, he saw the branches on the walls and the carpet of leaves beneath them. The bed they were in was circular and made of branches and twine, bearing an uncanny resemblance to a nest. On the table next to the bed were a note and his phone.

"We're going to be okay, Vee," was his vague reply.

He reached over for the phone to find it was fully charged with five bars. The flashing in the right-hand corner indicated two voice messages from unknown numbers. The note said:

Vanessa and Tom,
We hope you enjoyed your stay—and the show. Your El Dorado is parked outside with a full tank. It was a pleasure to meet you both.
Nevar.
PS. Needless to say, you were never here. Crows remember.

Vanessa peered through the branch-covered window to see the line of crow-people leading from the door to the car. Tom came up from behind—he had no intention of invading her space—but this was important. He hugged her close and whispered everything he had seen before losing consciousness.

He felt her pulse increase as the words landed and his words of comfort—"Stay strong. We are going home."—fell rather flat after the inconceivably macabre revelation.

Putting his phone on speaker, he played both messages, and together they listened to the confessions from Greg and Holly about a dead girl called Jessica.

For a while, they stayed close to each other, taking what comfort they could. It was too much to process at once; the entire experience too terrifying and surreal.

But they had to make a move—neither of them felt safe anymore.

They dressed in silence and walked outdoors into one almighty caw and a thundering cacophony of wings flapping and crow's feet tapping. Vanessa grabbed Tom's hand and nodded, and they made their way through the crowd back towards the El Dorado. As they approached, a crow flew directly over their heads and landed on the car's hood before cocking its head and looking directly at them. They stopped just short of the vehicle and, for a moment, watched the crow watching them. Another crow flew in from the right and landed. The first one squawked, then both flew away, and they watched as the crows headed down the hill, following the dirt path. Tom and Vanessa looked at each other and then got in the car.

"Tom, you need to wipe those messages," Vanessa said, her eyes watering. "I don't want to come back here as bird food."

So he did.

He suspected there'd come a moment when grief and shock would hit him, but, for the moment, he felt remarkably composed and optimistic under the circumstances. After all, he was sitting in his Dad's El Dorado with the one that fate chose.

"Can we go now, please?" Vanessa said.

"One second."

Tom opened the glove box and retrieved the lighter. He took the piece of crumpled card from his pocket and set fire to the crow's head, and they both watched as it burned. Then he started the engine and wheel-skidded away.

***

Never placed the note next to Jessica's photograph: a full confession from him, admitting sole responsibility for the deaths of Greg and Holly. An act of retribution.

The rest of the flock had already started dismantling everything, and soon any evidence they were ever there would be gone.

Finally, he could rest.

"Jessica," he said before putting the gun in his mouth and pulling the trigger.

Disconnect

The harsh red lines on the bedside clock warn me I only have one hour before I need to get up for work.

Here I am again, rigid and contorted in a way that suggests I don't want to sleep. My head is on the pillow, but it isn't resting. I am no longer comfortable, and I shift position and repeat the pattern, praying for sleep before the compulsive need to adjust inevitably sweeps over me again.

Elly sleeps so soundly. Her breathing is rhythmic and resentment-inducing.

I can only recall the first few lines of my pitch. Everyone will be there; it's a big one, could set me up for life. I can't bullshit through this one. No pressure. Elly has everything mapped out: a new house, private school for the kids, and a little beach house on the coast.

My eyes squelch like marshy ground as the balls of my hands bring a mixture of glorious relief and inevitable soreness. Black smudges appear against the greyness of diluted night as I release my hands and push myself from the deceitful softness of the bed. Dirty yellow light from the halogen outside spills through the side of the curtain, and I momentarily consider the possibility humans may eventually evolve to require no sleep at all.

I tiptoe to the bathroom being careful to avoid the squeaky floorboard, even though it would most likely not disturb. The devastation of countless sleepless nights stares back at me when I switch the light on, and it's even worse than I thought. My skin is pale and emphasises the darkness under my sunken eyes. I look like a clown with charcoal make-up. My eyes resemble an old yellowing road atlas, with branches of red lines that no longer reach their destination. My arms don't feel like my own as I reach for the cabinet door.

As I squeeze out an eye drop, my wife lets out a snort. I wonder how anyone could sleep so deeply that, even when their body erupts in such a way, steady breathing follows as though nothing has occurred. The envy burns again, and I am tempted to bang on the wall to show the injustice.

Nobody understands this affliction that steals my sleep. My mind is a melting pot of stress and worry that does not allow for luxuries such as relaxation. I imagine myself in the board room wearing my tired face, the puffy eyes and sallow skin further emphasised by the sharp lines of my suit. I watch myself choke as I float helplessly above. It's a miracle that I have evaded exposure for so long.

The twitch in my eye has already started, more violently than normal. My skin sings with irritation, and I lift my heavy arms and claw at the maddening patches of itch with bitten down fingernails.

I have always been a light sleeper, but this last year feels like a montage of out of body experiences, as though I am a spectator in my own unspectacular destruction. At work, I was both admired and despised for my work ethos and long nights in the office, but recently the work I have been turning in is patchy and half-hearted. I can't survive on reputation. Voices swim in and out during meetings, and I nod and hope nobody asks for an opinion. I can't bear anyone's company for more than five minutes without wanting to stab them in the eye. I am here, but not; a physical shell whose spark has left.

At home, I am the same. My kids have given up on me, and all I hear all day is the word Mummy. Elly has given up on me, too. I see it in her eyes. I have exhausted her with my own insomnia.

I've seen a hypnotist, a therapist, been on sleeping pills, tried alcohol and even cannabis, but it seems every new gimmick I attempt puts further distance between myself and the sleeping state. I can't find a way back.

I return to the bedroom with no intention of getting back into bed.

There is someone lying next to my wife.

My pulse quickens, and the bizarreness of the scene takes a while to settle in. For a moment, I assume I am dreaming, but that would mean I am asleep. I walk over to the edge of the bed, and it is myself I see nestled between the soft blankets. My eyes are closed, and I look peaceful. I look asleep.

I must be dreaming.

I might be okay for the pitch after all. Even a couple of hours would give me a shot.

Goose pimples tingle across my already sensitive skin as I reflect on the possibility of a breakthrough.

I am almost afraid to move. I don't want to overstimulate and bring myself out of this deep sleep. I reach out slowly to gently touch the top of my head, but my hand passes through, and I laugh out loud at the limitations of this absurd experience.

As I stand here bent over my physical form, I feel intensely present. The clock moves forward a minute as if to stamp the intricacy of the moment and then I hear the just-after-four o'clock slam of the car door across the road.

I watch the two of us in bed for some time. We lie as far apart as possible. Often in the old days, we would wake up a sweaty mass as though melding into one. I wonder when that stopped, when we gave up.

In our youth, we were ignorantly adamant that we were different from the rest. We mocked people who wanted the bigger house, the nice car, and two-point-four children, and now we are part of the game and it is tearing us apart. Elly used to be so passionate about her painting and I used to write until the early hours. It was all we seemed to need back then. And then we got sucked in like everyone else. Elly has bought into it in a big way, and we struggle to keep the pace with our so-called friends. It is exhausting but, ironically, insomnia-inducing.

I turn my attention to myself and feel utter loathing for the weak creature I have become. My face tells the tale of a beaten man, grey and exhausted, and, in the oversized antique bed, I look as vulnerable as a child.

I want the old us back, how we used to be when nothing else mattered. When we had passion. When life was not about collecting things.

I am lost in thought for some time and only shaken out of it by the sound of the alarm clock. Over an hour has passed.

"John."

There is no reaction from my physical self, and I do not feel any pull towards consciousness. My chest tightens—there is no way I would sleep through this.

Elly puts a hand on my shoulder and gives a gentle shove, but I feel nothing, and there is no sign this gesture is going to wake me. The alarm continues its annoying tune and Elly reaches over impatiently and switches it off.

"Come on, John, it's your big day today."

"I know," I reply.

"John."

I am suddenly very apprehensive about this situation.

"Did you take a pill?" she asks.

She doesn't wait for a response but walks to the bathroom and sits down on the toilet.

"Wake up," I scream in my ear.

I have a pitch to deliver in less than two hours and if I don't do it, that dickhead Harvey will.

With eyes closed tightly, I imagine myself waking up, but it feels futile. The process should be automatic, but I don't have a blueprint on how to get back.

She comes back into the room wearing the familiar frown. "Are you ignoring me, John? John!"

The shriek of her voice sends my eye twitching again. Hello, anxiety, old friend.

"Wake up, you idiot," I scream.

"This isn't funny, John. Wake up!" she follows.

My physical form shows no signs of waking, and I feel no draw back into the real world. I grab a fold of skin under my arm and pinch hard. It hurts—a lot—but again there is no sign of a reaction. Elly starts to shake me, quite vigorously, and I watch my head stupidly lollop around on the pillow. A little bit of saliva drops down the side of my mouth. She coils her hand back to slap me and I close my eyes and brace myself for impact, but nothing comes. When I open my eyes, I see the red mark on the cheek of my physical self, and the detachment scares me.

If this is not a dream, perhaps I am dead. Instinctively, I want to hug my children, Tom and Anne, and tell them I'm sorry. The last words I spat at them were to be quiet and go and watch TV. If I am dead, they will grow up to remember me as a nasty and short-tempered man. This is not who I am or aspire to be, but insomnia has stolen my identity. My beautiful children—I have to get back and put this right.

Elly reaches for my pulse and, at the same time, I put my head to my chest. Relief kicks in as I hear and feel my heart continuing to do its job.

Elly picks up the phone, and I feel a certain satisfaction as I sense her anguish. The worry lines age her immediately, and I see weakness, a vulnerable side that rarely shows its face. I want to hold her and tell her I'll do better. Perhaps she does still care.

"I think I need an ambulance. My husband won't wake up."

There is urgency in her voice. I don't think the beach house is on her mind, at least I hope not.

"… breathing fine, slow, but the pulse is there."

Her eyes are getting moist. She looks like she may cry.

"I've tried, but nothing. Please come."

There it is, a solitary tear rolling down her cheek.

I watch her announce our address over the phone and, in an instant, she is back to reliable and professional Elly. The lawyer in her is taking over again, and the vulnerability is gone.

It was good to see that side of her, albeit briefly.

She puts the phone down and places her hand on my cheek. "Come on, John. Time to wake up now."

"I'm trying, Elly."

She pushes herself from the bed, opens her wardrobe, and throws some clothes onto a nearby chair. The phone is nestled into her neck as she slips on her jeans and informs the office she won't be in today.

Work—I almost forgot. Suddenly, I find myself running through my pitch, and it has all come back to me. I feel alert, present, and I know I could pull it off. Ethan, my boss, will text soon to make sure I get in early. I need to get back. Come on, wake up, for God's sake!

I watch her dress efficiently and then she checks on me again: still sleeping. The hospital is only a few minutes away. Elly insisted on being central, in the bustle of city madness. We stare out the window side by side and wait for the ambulance to arrive. I have no idea what is going to happen next.

It arrives without the sirens—still early enough for traffic to be sparse. Two men step out with alacrity, and they open the rear doors and retrieve a stretcher. It is all happening so fast. I want to wake up.

Elly rushes downstairs, and I'm left in the company of my sleeping self. I hear the whistle of the birds outside, and I can see the trees rustle in the breeze. A plastic bag journeys erratically from one side of the road to the other and adds to the realism of the moment.

Everything feels too tangible to be a dream.

"Christ, wake up," I scream.

I close my eyes and try to come back once more, but I feel too present. The front door opens, followed by the march of feet up the stairs. I try once more, but it's no good. It's as if I have disconnected.

My wife answers their questions. Her tired and monotone descriptions indicate they're the same questions asked on the phone.

I watch as they carry my body away. In the background, I can hear Elly talking to her mum, asking her to come and look after the kids. Elly's Mum is only five minutes away. Another perk of being central— at least today.

I follow Elly and the men carrying my stretchered body through the front door. The breeze feels incredibly real, and for a moment I kid myself the sensation of the cool prickle on my skin might bring me back, but then I see the faded red mark on my cheek from where Elly slapped me, and the thought fades quickly.

Our neighbour, Joan, has come outside to see what is going on. I flick her the middle finger and utter "Nosey old bag" as I step into the van behind myself. My body is rigid with panic as I watch our street disappear through the ambulance window. This is as real as it gets.

The journey to the hospital is short, and it isn't long before they wheel my body out of the ambulance. The sound of approaching sirens can be heard, and again I optimistically hope the shrill sound will bring me back from whatever this is. As we make our way through the doors, I turn around to see the paramedics pull a body from the ambulance, and even from a distance, I can see the blood and the ripped clothing, the head still encased in the helmet.

I feel lightheaded. My tick is going crazy. The clinical décor of the hospital is grounding, yet I am struggling to keep the pace. Everything is happening so quickly, and all I can think about is Tom and Anne and how much I've let them down. I wonder if they're worried about me, if they care at all about the grumpy train wreck of a father that I have become.

The doctor gives me the once over, and I'm then taken to a room full of machines. He makes some notes before leaving, and I watch as the nurse places tubes into my arm and connects me to multiple contraptions. I feel nothing.

Elly holds my hand — I can't remember the last time she did. Life seems too fast for that. She looks frail again, off guard. I wish I could feel her touch.

I find this scene difficult to watch, and I can't get enough air; the seriousness of the situation feels suffocating. I'm struggling to maintain the conviction that I will soon wake up in bed next to Elly. Every minute I'm out of my body, it feels as though the distance back to it is growing. The serious faces, the frowns and chin stroking, the beeps from the machine and announcements on the speaker system all add to my growing sense of dread. I need someone to come and sort me out. Where has the doctor gone? Why isn't anyone helping me?

I run out of the room into the corridor and scream, "Where are all the fucking doctors?"

Of course, there is no reaction.

"I think that might be my fault, champ," the unexpected reply belatedly echoes down the corridor.

There are a couple of nurses urgently marching from one room to another and a patient pushing their bag on a pole; an electrician is changing one of the lights in the ceiling and on the other side of the ladders stands a guy wearing a motorcycle helmet and ripped leathers. He is holding his right hand in the air as if we are old friends with a prearrangement to meet.

He starts walking over. I say walk, but it's more of a swagger, as though he hasn't a care in the world. My legs feel weak, but I make my way towards him. I wonder how he can see me, but I'm more curious as to how he could be here when he was so obviously broken and laid out on a stretcher when I saw him outside.

"Luke," he says as he holds out his hand.

He seems unmarked, contrary to the state of his clothing.

"I'm dying," he says in an eerily matter-of-fact tone.

"I'm John," I reply and hold out my hand just as he moves his away.

"The doctors are trying to bring me back, but it's too late, and I think they know it, too," he says.

I suppose I should offer some consolation, but I can only think about my own fate. Am I dying, too?

"What's your story?" he asks as he removes his helmet. "And how can you see me?"

"I'm asleep," I reply.

He looks at me puzzled for a moment and then smiles and says, "My body is smashed up, and my brain is bleeding. I'm on my way to the next one and doubt it will be pretty. And you say you're asleep?"

His face is full of deep cavernous lines, and his nose is twisted out of shape; it tells the story of a hard life. There are cuts to his face that would be hard to replicate with a handheld razor, but no sign of major head trauma.

"I can't wake up. I've tried, but I think I'm in a coma or something — I don't know. We're waiting for the doctors."

He looks at me and smiles. "What are the odds?"

This line sounds strange to me and triggers my instincts to high alert. "What do you mean?"

"I just mean it's a bizarre situation, the two of us talking here like this when our bodies lie elsewhere. "

He's right, of course. It is a strange situation. But my gut instincts compel me to get away from this man as quickly as possible. We have nothing in common apart from our misfortune, and I instantly decided he wasn't friend material from the way he initially swaggered over.

"Are you married? Kids?" he asks.

"I am, and I should be getting back to her — and me."

He's still smiling, and I find it rather unsettling. There's no acknowledgement that lets me go easily, just an awkward pause as he continues to study my face. I am sure he knows how uncomfortable he is making me feel.

I start to back away, and the words feel weak when they leave my lips, "I'm truly sorry about your circumstance, perhaps they will fix you — bring you back?"

Another awkward silence as I continue my polite retreat.

"The thing is, John, I don't really want to come back — not as him anyway. Luke has a whole heap of trouble waiting for him. "

The immediate reference to himself in third-party escalates my fear.

His smile fades and he takes a step forward. "So why can't you just climb back inside, friend?"

It's a good question, but I don't want to discuss this with him. It's a question I have asked myself many times over the last few hours, and the only conclusion I can draw is that I have forgotten how to. I feel lost in limbo between wakefulness and sleep, and the disconnection is terrifying.

"I have to get back, Luke. Good luck," I say as I turn, walk, and then begin to run.

It's a bizarre situation to feel so much panic without feeling any elevated energy in those around. The nurses continue their daily chores and the patients are wandering about, bored, and lonely. I instinctively want to call for help but know it will do me no good. My feet noiselessly stomp on the floor, and I inhale the disinfectant-laced air as I weave in and out of objects that I could most likely run straight through.

I check behind. He's not there, but I don't stop running. I want to put as much distance between us as possible.

It wouldn't work. It can't be as simple as that.

Finally, I reach the room, and everything is as I left it. Elly still has hold of my hand.

My body is rigid with fear and anger. I haven't been on my game, but I don't deserve this.

I want another chance to do better, to be happier, and I want to sit down with her and tell her everything I was too afraid to before. We could reset, start again—get back to what's important.

I close my eyes and imagine myself floating through a black chasm towards the light. It seems to be working and, slowly, the tension begins to drain from my body. I am beginning to feel weightless and far removed from the clinical surrounds of the hospital. The sounds from the machines fade and voices begin to echo around me, and as I reach towards the light, I see my wife beckoning me to keep going.

I'm almost there, and I am beginning to feel her delicate hands on mine and the gentle pressure. I hear Elly scream from impossibly far away, "He moved! Nurse!"

So close to the light.

I stretch out my arm and I'm already preparing for the transition back to my physical self. And then suddenly, I am frozen, suspended in darkness. I feel something tight around my throat and I begin the freefall back into nothingness.

I can hardly breathe as I open my eyes. I know the two hands around my neck belong to Luke. The smell of cheap aftershave and leather permeates the air. I grab his wrists and try and prize them away, but I have no strength. I am weak and tired and can already feel my body shutting down. I was so cl—

***

I hear voices and commotion as I begin to come around. Momentarily, I convince myself I am in the hospital bed and finally awakening from this nightmare. But I am not, I am lying on the floor where Luke left me after choking me out.

The nurse tries to convince my wife to make me stay, but Luke is already familiarising himself with my body as he slips on my pants and shirt. She is insisting that more tests are needed, but he grabs Elly's hand and heads for the door. As he is about to push through, he stops and turns to Elly and asks for a pen. She looks at him oddly but obliges. He picks up the newspaper from the table and looks up thoughtfully for a moment before scribbling something and throwing the paper on the bed.

And then they are gone.

I am alone. More alone than I have ever been and more alone than anyone should ever be. I'm a spectator once again but even more so now. The thought is unbearable—I cannot be an audience in my own life.

My only escape lies in a room somewhere in this hospital. I hope I'm not too late, and I pray that I can slip into the broken body and drift peacefully away.

On my way out of the room, I glance at the writing scrawled across the newspaper:

You snooze, you lose.

The Necklace

She woke up to see the old lady sitting in the chair.

"How are you feeling, dear?" the white-haired stranger asked, and placed the magazine she was reading down on the table.

As she slowly pushed herself up, Cassie rubbed her eyes and took a closer look at the lady at the end of the bed. Her face was kind but certainly well-worn, and the deep cavernous valleys in her forehead suggested an anything-but-ordinary life. The old lady's sunken eyes were still a beautiful blue, surrounded by wrinkles decades in the making. Dry, frizzy white hair sporadically sprouted from the mostly bald scalp.

Cassie thought her to be the oldest person she had ever seen.

"I have a headache; could you pass me some water please?" Cassie finally asked.

"Of course, dear," the old lady answered before raising herself out of the chair.

Cassie's first thought was how nimble she was for an oldie. It was only when the lady passed her the glass that she noticed the cruelly misshapen fingers.

No wonder her face reads so traumatically.

"It's good to meet you, Cassie. I've heard a lot about you."

"Good to meet you, too," she replied, still hazy. "Sorry, who are you?"

The old lady laughed. "My name is Edith, dear. Just think of me as unpaid help."

Cassie shrugged and gulped a mouthful of water down. "Could you pass me the hairbrush, please?"

The old lady gave her an odd look at first before noticing the small mirror on the back of the brush. She grabbed it and held it a few inches in front of Cassie. The shock of her reflection was history, but losing her hair was still an upsetting step towards the alienation she felt from others. Every time she saw herself, Cassie was reminded that she'd once spent ages standing in front of the mirror cussing at the tangles. She'd give anything to have it back now. After running her hand over the smoothness of her scalp, she applied a thin layer of lipstick to her pale lips. Her dad had brought in the wrong shade of red, but it was better than nothing.

"It doesn't take long these days," she joked.

Edith smiled. "Do you want to play a game or watch some television, perhaps?"

"No thanks, Edith. I prefer to read. I can escape into someone else's life then," she said and half smiled. "Could you give me a quick hand with this pillow?"

As Edith leaned over, Cassie prepared for a blast of old lady smell—one that always reminded her of the sugared almonds that her mum used to buy before cancer took her. But strangely there was no scent, neither good nor bad.

It was then that she took notice of the necklace that dangled from the old lady's scaly neck and the deep blue light that emanated from the crystal. It pulsated, like a living breathing organism. She thought it was the most beautiful thing she'd ever seen. Instinctively, she reached for it, but the old lady grasped her wrist with incredible speed, not aggressively, but enough to stun Cassie and make her feel about six years old. Edith maintained her smile and composure throughout, as though a thousand people before Cassie had done the same thing. Finally, she released the girl's hand before undoing the clasp of her necklace and gently placing the crystal around Cassie's neck.

Cassie smiled at the old lady before reaching for the mirror again. The crystal sat nicely on her neck and offered some colour to the pallid skin that surrounded it. Admiringly, she ran her fingers over the stone and its faint blue glow.

"It suits you," Edith said. "There's more to it, though, Cassie. A lot more."

Cassie frowned. "What do you mean?"

"That crystal could save your life," Edith said casually.

Cassie looked unimpressed. Regardless of intention, the words felt nonsensical and almost cruel, and she immediately started to feel uncomfortable. Small talk was one thing, but when dotty old strangers started to spin tales about the power of crystals, it was time to bail. She didn't want to come across as rude or ungrateful, so she said politely, "The doctors have said it's too far gone, Edith. There is nothing else they can do."

"Cassie, the stone around your neck is more than a crystal. It is ancient, a relic from times long gone. Not only does it measure the wearer's life source, but it attracts other people's, too. Once someone touches the crystal, their life source will flow to you."

Cassie was beginning to feel a wave of heaviness approaching. Most of her day was spent in and out of bed, an endless cycle of drugs and exhaustion, and this old lady's gibberish wasn't something she could cope with right now. It was time for sleep, time for the crystal lady to leave.

"Edith, thanks for visiting, but I would like to get some rest now. Can you please take the necklace off and perhaps come back another time?"

The old lady nodded and smiled before undoing the clasp of the necklace and helping Cassie's head onto the pillow. "Sure," she said. But before Edith left, she crouched next to the bed and softly whispered into Cassie's ear, "You have three days left, dear."

***

She woke up in immense pain, and it took an agonising few seconds to get her bearings and to push the red button. Linda rushed in and, after taking one look at her patient, turned on the daily dose of morphine. "Beautiful necklace," she said matter-of-factly, nodding towards the bedside table.

Cassie looked down to see the crystal on the table refracting the crisp fluorescent light from the hospital ceiling. She'd forgotten about the visit.

"The old lady gave it to me. Edith?" she said, as she swung her leg over the edge of the bed.

"Go careful, Cassie. Slow down. Who's Edith?"

"Damn."

The pain was worse than usual this morning. It seemed more concentrated, as though she could feel it pushing against her bones.

Three days. Had Edith really said that? But that can't be true. The doctors said I have weeks, possibly months.

The feeling of her insides being on fire, though, leaned more towards the old lady's diagnosis.

No, please, this can't be happening.

"Linda, I need more morphine."

"Cassie, you had your allocated amount this morning. I can't give you more. You'll be as high as a kite."

"The necklace then, please."

Linda sighed, but diligently collected it from the table and then gently placed it around her neck. Once again Cassie admired the faint light blue glow, but could not help wishing for something brighter.

"Bathroom, Linda," she said, grimacing through the pain.

As she was wheeled through the corridor, she heard the other children's voices and laughter coming from the lounge area.

Three days.

Linda held the door to the bathroom open and Cassie manoeuvred herself through. Every muscle burned, and even moving a few feet was exhausting, but it was only when the door closed behind her that she let herself cry.

After flicking off the light, she stood in front of the large mirror that ran the full length of the wall. The light from the crystal only generated a small amount of luminescence, enough for her face to glow, but the rest of the room was mostly in darkness.

She studied the necklace carefully and thought about what the old lady said, and then about her dad and what it would mean to him if she could recover, or even buy some time—be it days, weeks, or perhaps even years.

Didn't Edith say it could even save my life? At the expense of what though?

She thought of her ballet and how far she might have been able to take it, and she thought of all the books she could read during the long summers without the cloud of death hanging over her.

A hypothetical conversation with her dad started to play out in her head, and she wondered how he would react, especially after losing Mum to cancer already. Would he condemn such a selfish and immoral action or would he be so desperate to keep her alive that he would give his blessing?

God, I miss you, Mum.

As she pondered, the crystal began to flicker erratically—quickly at first, but then it slowed to a weak pulse. The time that elapsed between light and dark gradually began to increase until there were long and uncomfortable spans of complete and terrifying darkness. Cassie started to panic; she wasn't ready to go yet. She rubbed the crystal frantically with her fingers as though she could jump start it with some left-over juice stored for emergencies. But it didn't help. The room started to spin, and her legs felt like jelly. She backed up and steadied herself against the side of the cubicle before sliding down and wrapping her arms around her knees.

And then, finally, the light flickered and reverted to its familiar constant dull glow.

And she sobbed. For herself. For her parents. For her pain. And for what she was about to do.

After wiping the tears from her swollen eyes and taking a deep breath, she shouted to Linda that she was ready and was wheeled into the lounge and to her newly found friendship group of dying kids.

"Oh, my goodness, that is gorgeous," Josie gushed as she leaned in to take a closer look. Cassie instinctively flinched away.

"Calm down, Cassie. I just want to look."

She looked at Josie, and momentarily, it was the face of her father staring back. And just like that, any remaining doubt faded. Cassie leaned into her and let the necklace dangle freely.

"Where did you get this from?" Josie asked.

"From Edith, the old lady that visits."

"Edith? Well, she is one generous woman!"

Josie reached across, and as soon as she caressed the crystal, it emitted a sky-blue light, much stronger than its previous pale radiance, accompanied by an immediate surge through Cassie's body that felt like a very mild electric shock. Hardly noticeable relative to the constant pain that terrorised her, but something, nonetheless.

"Wow, how does that work?" Josie laughed. She released it and watched as it faded back to a paler light.

"It's one of those mood crystals," Cassie said, almost impressed with how quickly the lie came to her lips.

"Can I try it on?"

"Sorry, Josie, not today."

"Let's have a go," Max shouted as he snatched at the crystal. The stone immediately illuminated, sending another surge of energy through her body—stronger this time; much stronger than with Josie. She jolted, but Max didn't notice. He was too smitten by the crystals' glow. As she watched the blue light bounce off his eyes, she wondered how long he had left.

More than Josie, but how long?

"Enough," she screamed, as she grabbed his wrist and pulled it away from the stone, feeling a combination of guilt and the sensation that someone was running a blunt knife down the centre of her chest. Heads turned and the room went immediately quiet. Max looked sad. His bottom lip started to quiver uncontrollably until finally his tears came.

"I'm sorry, Max." *For everything.*

She thrashed at her wheels but couldn't get away quick enough. "Linda," she yelled and was quickly escorted back to her room. As she was carefully hoisted back onto the bed, the pain continued to rip through her with ever-increasing intensity. She screamed in agony and gripped the metal guards until her fingers were almost translucently white. The metallic taste of blood followed as she bit down hard on her lip. In the background, she could hear Linda calling for assistance, but the voice was suddenly distorted and distant as though coming from way above. Her body writhed in agony, an unbearable searing pain like nothing she had felt before—as if someone had stuck their hand into her chest and was squeezing her organs. For a moment, she thought she might pass out, that she could take no more, but then she felt the pain start to subside—no doubt from the dose of morphine that Linda would have mercifully administered.

Something had gone wrong. Perhaps the crystal didn't work properly. But she'd seen its radiance and felt the exchange. Shutting her eyes tightly, she pictured her dad and how devastated he would be if she left now. *I don't understand. Why is this happening to me?*

The voice of the old lady replied, "It was a test, Cassie."

She opened her eyes and saw Edith sitting at the end of the bed.

"You're back," Linda said.

"Can you see her?" Cassie gasped.

"Who, Cassie?" Linda replied.

"Edith," she said, but didn't have the energy to lift her arm.

"Cassie, you've just had morphine, love. The doctor's on his way. Try to relax."

"Please take it off," Cassie said. "The necklace. Please take it off!"

"It's too late, Cassie," Edith interjected.

"Take it off," she screamed.

"Okay, okay," Linda appeased, and she unclasped the necklace and draped it across the bedside table.

Cassie craned her neck to watch the sporadic flicker of pale light emanating from the crystal. The pulse was becoming slower. She felt the darkness creeping in, as though someone was dimming the lights of the hospital room. The world was washing away.

Then she was sitting on the end of the bed next to Edith, watching as her body gently faded away.

"Edith? What's happening to me?"

"You're dying, Cassie. You are passing."

"Edith, I'm scared."

The old lady reached across for her palm, and Cassie couldn't believe her eyes as the silky-smooth skin of Edith's hand and long elegant fingers wrapped around hers.

"Edith—"

It didn't stop with her hands. The old lady's skin was changing, rejuvenating. Sagging skin was tightening. Age spots were fading.

Cassie began to feel the heat from the woman's hand leaking into hers, getting hotter all the time, and when she tried to break free, the hand over hers clasped even tighter.

"It was a test, Cassie. And you failed." The voice had changed, too. Deep and guttural. Otherworldly.

The face was next as the ancient cliffs that dominated the forehead slowly began to collapse, giving way to flawlessly smooth skin. Cheeks filled out and loose skin under the eyes disappeared. Long dark hair covered the scalp in seconds, thick and glossy and intensely black.

From the corner of her eye, Cassie saw the doctor rush through the door and towards her still body, but couldn't take her eyes from the transformation that was taking place. Voices floated across the room but never seemed to reach her. It was as if they were on a different plane—another world.

The old lady was gone. Something else had taken her place. Cassie's first thought was of beauty, but there was something innately ugly about this new version: a cold and calculating stare that made the hair prickle on the back of her neck. As the eyes began to change, blue faded to black, and black to fiery red. Within them, she could see bodies writhing in pain, contorted but alive, an endless sea of fire and tortured souls whose mouths were opened so wide she could almost hear them screaming.

"A deal is a deal, Cassie." That voice again.

"What are you talking about?" she cried. "I never made any deal."

She felt something digging into her wrist and briefly glanced down to see sharp black fingernails beginning to coil around her. They smouldered like hot tar and, impossibly quickly, they began to snake up Cassie's arm.

"But I did, with your so-called God, Cassie. He had faith in you. He has misplaced faith in you all."

"I don't understand," Cassie said.

The black nails started to wrap around her chest, the burning sensation increasing steadily.

"The necklace works in reverse. You were prepared to suck the life from others, Cassie, even young children. God said you would pass, but I knew better. And sometimes we wager to relieve the boredom."

"You … you deceived me?" Cassie's voice quivered.

"And you deceived them."

"So you are the Devil?" She sobbed.

"Indeed, Cassie. And you are coming with me."

Cassie looked away, tearing herself from the scenes that played out in the Devil's eyes.

Soon she would have to call that home.

She thought of her parents, her friends, and everything she would miss. *Wouldn't anyone do what they could to get extra time with their loved ones?*

The sound came, a piercing slow-motion high-pitched drone that she knew represented the end of her life. If she looked, she would see the machine displaying a continuous horizontal green line. Instead, she eyed the dull crystal on the table and willed it to flash, as though there might be a chance of it starting up again—like in the bathroom. But it sat cold and lifeless—like her body.

The black fingernails consumed her now in a thick, impenetrable cocoon.

The Devil reached for the necklace with its other hand.

Before they both crumbled to ashes, Cassie heard, "At least you can say hello to your mum."

The Finishing Line

Friday

Jack was acutely aware that he had reached a stage in his life that offered no mercy.

Saturday

Jack found himself sitting in the bath, crying. It wasn't because the water was too hot; he was severely depressed and didn't have a clue how he was going to drag himself out of it. It was the first time he had bathed and not showered for over twenty years, but here he was, sitting in his own diluted filth, the fingers of his right hand curled around the handle of the Stanley knife.

The sudden breakdown was most likely brought on by Dean, not a friend exactly, but someone he had known for some time. Their paths crossed when their partners dragged them to the same social soiree's that made them both feel even more at odds with the rest of humanity. It became apparent very quickly they were very alike; superficially, they could just about pass for human beings with all the pleasantries and small talk, but inwardly—if he was right about Dean—they were both as volatile as a volcano, ready to spill out on everything around with an unstoppable eruption of suppressed emotion. It turned out he was right about Dean, whose suicide last week hadn't surprised Jack at all.

Their lives had been almost identical. They were both married and lived in the same part of the country with similar professions and two kids. They were introverted, intelligent, caught in the rat race, and admitted to each other they were engaging in a lifestyle set by other people's expectations. At forty-four years of age, stuck in a dead-end job with a mortgage and two kids to put through college, he wondered where it all went wrong. A hundred or so years ago he would already most likely be dead at that age, and just as he would have started thinking he'd had enough, he would have perished with impeccable timing—a great escape.

On paper, he had a great life, but something was missing. He knew he had no right to feel that way considering the world's struggles with illness and famine and so forth, and it wasn't that he was ungrateful exactly, just not happy. He tried many times to reset himself but couldn't fake it. Depression, by all accounts, couldn't be cured, and today was a testament to that.

Sunday

Jack was out the door early. He liked to get out first thing as there was less chance of seeing other people. He ran at least six kilometres daily, and often a lot more. Exercise for him was meditation. He ran without music other than the soundtrack of the birds and the rustle of the trees in the breeze. He saw dozens of eagles as he ran on his favourite trail, and he imagined them looking down on him and mocking his spindly way of moving as they glided effortlessly across the sky. He wanted to be an eagle. He was jealous of their freedom to take off and fly far away.

A few minutes into his run, just as he had started to survey the surroundings of the open land either side of the railway track, he experienced a feeling of disappointment as he saw the distant figure running towards him. The closer the person got, the more it looked like Dean. But it couldn't be him, of course. Dean had been found hanging from a tree in his back garden. With about twenty yards between them, he realised it *was* Dean. The dead man nonchalantly uttered "Hi" as he ran by. The brief greeting did not surprise Jack; that would have been the norm for Dean. What was unsettling was the fact that he'd seemingly arisen from the grave. He shouted after him but recalled the earphones Dean had been wearing. Jack stood for a moment, wondering if he'd gone stark raving mad. It crossed his mind that it might have been a hallucinatory vision brought on by his depression. The fact that he had called after Dean and put his lack of response down to him having earphones in and not the fact he was dead was an alarm bell.

He didn't finish his run. He went home to have breakfast with his family. He thought about telling his wife but decided against it and looked up depression again on the internet instead. Ironically, it was under his favourite saved searches. It was some comfort to him that there was an abundance of credible sources offering various solutions and advice. On the other hand, the discovery that so many people in the world were depressed was like watching a news programme that reported only the bad news. He clicked on depressive psychosis, but within minutes it had started to make him even more upset, so he refilled his coffee and went back to feeling invisible at the breakfast table.

Both kids were on their iPads and his wife was on the laptop. He wondered when it had become acceptable for such behavior to be an everyday occurrence, and if there was some correlation between the growing number of suicides and the lack of emotional connection brought on by people's attachment to their devices. He wondered a lot of things but rarely reached any startling conclusions.

"Dad."

"*Dad*," his son Daniel shouted at him.

"Err, yeah. What's up, Dan?"

"I need a lift to Phil's house."

Jack moved his leg to the side to get up from the table but collapsed to the floor in a heap, his leg offering no support whatsoever. He had moved it and saw it move, but it was as though it wasn't there. Daniel laughed so hard he went red in the face, and Emily, his nine-year-old daughter, looked at him and shook her head. His wife, Ruth, glanced up from her laptop and softly asked, "Are you okay, Jack?"

He wanted to scream at the top of his lungs that he wasn't okay and to rip the tablecloth from the table. He wanted to pour water from the kettle over all the electronic devices at the table. But most of all, he wanted the ground to open up and swallow him whole.

"Fine, thanks," he replied.

He dropped Daniel off at his friend's house and drove to the pier to stare at the water. It seemed like ten minutes to Jack, but when he glanced at his watch, he realised he'd sat watching the water for over two hours.

Where to from here?

He began beating the steering wheel and bit down on his lip so hard he drew blood. Next came a howl like a wild dog's, and it felt good, an animalistic reaction to conformity and all the chains that society had managed to lock him in over the years. He imagined them breaking as he transformed into a wild beast—a predator and not prey. He screamed and pounded his fists on the dashboard and seat, and his spittle sprayed across the windscreen. The calm of the water did nothing to tame the beast that he was becoming. Jack was lost in the transformation long enough for the couple in the car to pull up next to him and then quickly depart once they set eyes on the apparent lunatic, assumedly high on something, and thrashing away to some obscure heavy metal track. Eventually, he calmed. His heart rate dropped, and he was Jack once again, hair slightly ruffled and with sore palms and lips, but he was back, no sign of the beast.

Sunday p.m.

As he poured himself a whisky, he thought back to the previous events and laughed. The laughter soon turned into hysterics and, before long, he was in tears.

"What's so funny?" Ruth asked, smiling.

"Everything, Ruth, and nothing," he said.

Ruth looked at him, frowned, and smiled before going back to her screen.

His phone on the table started to vibrate. He was due to travel down with his boss to an exhibition the next day, and no doubt Colin wanted to talk strategy.

Colin can suck my—

"Are you going to answer that?" Ruth asked.

Jack reached for it and watched his hand pass straight through the surface of the small table and through the phone. He tried again, and the same thing happened.

What the hell?

"Ruth, watch this!"

The table went clattering over and the phone skimmed across the wooden floor for a good ten yards before coming to rest near Ruth's feet.

"Impressive." Ruth scowled.

Jack downed his whisky and decided he would not be going to work tomorrow, as he was going slowly, but surely, psychotic.

"Ruth," he said, on the verge of spilling everything.

"What now? Are you going to throw the couch out the window?"

"I'm going to bed," Jack announced resignedly.

He sent a text to Colin explaining he was not feeling well and would not be fit for tomorrow. He undressed, put his pyjamas on, and walked into the bathroom. It wasn't until he sat down on the toilet that he suddenly realised he hadn't caught his reflection in the mirror. Adamant he must have missed it, he slowly shuffled towards the mirror, covering his manhood with his hands.

Oh, shit.

"Ruth, come here now!"

"I have to finish this for tomorrow, Jack, can't it wait?"

"No, it most certainly cannot. Please come here now."

He heard her walking up the stairs, and when she arrived outside the bathroom, he asked her if she could see his reflection. She looked towards the mirror and then back at Jack and then towards the mirror again. "Jack, yes, I can see your reflection. What the hell is going on?"

He wanted to grab her and pull her close, to let himself sink into her embrace and nestle into the warmth of her neck but thought he would most likely break down and start bawling like a baby. His pride prevented him from seeking such comfort. *Pride—the devil's sin.*

Instead, he looked back towards the mirror, and some relief kicked in as he saw his frail, grey, wrinkly, but visible, reflection.

"Do you want me to run you a bath? Put some candles on, perhaps?"

"Christ, no," he said. "I think I'll just read for a bit. Are you coming to bed?"

Jack switched the bedside light on and reached for his book. Again, his hand passed straight through the cover. The same on the second attempt. Finally, on the third effort, he managed to grab it.

He considered the day's events: the Dean sighting, the breakfast table episode, his hand seemingly passing through solid objects, and the lack of reflection in the bathroom mirror. Something was happening to him. He had no idea what, but it had certainly got his attention. It all started after the bath on Saturday. He'd decided he was going to kill himself on Friday night when Ruth and the kids were visiting her mum. He was going to use a Stanley knife, but, instead, he had sat and blubbered. The thought did cross his mind that he might have actually done it and that he was already dead, and how that might explain seeing Dean on Saturday. It might even help explain the lack of reflection and the limbs that seemingly lost their molecular structure at times.

I'm losing my bloody mind!

He put his book down after reading three words and allowed himself to move in behind his wife and was glad he could feel her, the warmth, the presence, and the solidity. He drifted into a tormented sleep, waking up twice and checking his reflection both times.

Monday

Jack was struggling to cope with the familiar Monday morning turmoil. He turned his attention to his daughter, a shining light in his otherwise dreary existence—always singing and invariably smiling. He watched her brushing her hair and wrestling with the tangles, singing as usual, with seemingly not a care in the world. How he wished that could always be the case for her.

Ruth kissed him on the cheek and told him to get some rest. Before she left with the kids, she also suggested booking an appointment to see the doctor. It was the first time he had been left in the house on his own for some time, and he had a strange feeling that, at that moment in time, he was temporarily not part of anything, a feeling that was perfectly fine with him.

Within minutes, the emptiness and quiet gave way to the dark thoughts, and he decided he needed to get out. He'd go for a long run. He looked at himself in the bathroom mirror, relieved to see his reflection, and splashed some water on his face before putting his running gear on. He managed to grab his shoes only on the second attempt, but didn't dwell on that.

The morning mist was still lurking, and it created a stunning view over the fields as the sun did its bit to raise Monday morning morale. Jack settled into his pace quickly and took deep gulps of air as he enjoyed the scenery and watched the rabbits duck and dive into their holes.

And then Dean emerged into view, just visible over the next hillock.

Jack felt a change in the air: it got chillier, and the sun no longer provided the warmth on his cheek. The light was fading quickly as though the sun had decided against it that day after all.

As Dean drew closer, Jack saw the makeshift noose around his neck. From a distance, it had looked like a scarf, but now he could also see the swollen red line across his neck and the bloodshot eyes brought on by asphyxiation.

"Don't fight it," Dean whispered as he ran by and gave a smile, tugging at his neck scarf.

Jack carried on running. His pace accelerated, and his heart pumped faster. A bolt of lightning struck the ground metres behind him, and the subsequent thunderous sound shook the ground and almost sent him off into the verge. He afforded himself a second to look up at the sky, and it had fast become an apocalyptic setting of darkness. Huge foreboding clouds, interspersed with bright orange volcanic swirls, sent down lightning bolts towards him with sinister accuracy.

He glanced behind and caught sight of a shape approaching in the distance. It was too dark to make out the form, but he heard an accompanying, predatory growl, and that was enough for him to face forwards. He was already flat out and breathing hard, and his body was telling him to stop, but fear was propelling him onwards. Panic set in and he turned his head again and saw the pursuer in more detail: part human and part animal with a shiny black body and four muscly legs with hooves that were galloping beginning to close in. Its black pointed tail flicked viciously behind like a sleek leathery whip, and its red eyes were bearing down on him. Two large horns protruded from the top of its head, and they looked poised to strike.

Jack's foot skimmed some of the foliage on the side of the path, and he stumbled but managed to catch his balance. He faced forward again and could feel his legs were close to giving out. A bolt of lightning barely missed him to the left, and he heard the ground sizzle. The thunder that followed was bone-shaking.

His heart began to beat unbearably fast. As he looked down, he couldn't see his feet or legs. They were missing. He could feel his feet pounding on the ground, but they were no longer visible, and the disorientation almost sent him stumbling off the edge of the track once again. Meanwhile, the sound of the hooves on the ground behind him intensified. The odds had been against him from the start, and he felt himself giving up and slowing down. A fleeting sensation of relief swept over him as he prepared himself for the end. He stopped running, closed his eyes, and hoped it would be quick.

"Daddy, run!"

The voice in his head was his daughter's, and a spike of adrenaline surged through him. He opened his eyes and could see her where she stood at a finishing line that had materialised in the distance. She smiled and waved, and he waved back.

Behind him, the beast had stopped its gallop and sauntered towards him, believing the battle won. Its giant paws silently padded the ground and its tail flickered excitedly from side to side. Its eyes glowed like red-hot stones, and a deep panting sound came from a mouth that unveiled four rows of pointed teeth on the lower jaw. A huge barbed forked tongue protruded and slowly licked the air as though tasting his fear.

Jack was transfixed by the creature's eyes; the orange glow coupled with the rhythmic sway of the sleek black body had a hypnotic effect that was almost comforting. Jack felt his heart rate slow. His gaze was still fixed on the red eyes, but he could see in the background the tail rising upwards and the scorpion-like stinger that was being hoisted into the air. For a moment, he was paralysed.

"Run!" The scream came from behind him.

He turned and saw his entire family at the finishing line, and even Daniel was animated and screaming encouragement. Ruth was on her knees, crying.

"Run, Daddy," Emily screamed.

Another shot of adrenaline poured through him and he slowly moved his feet and started to back away. The tail was at full height and hovered above him, ready to flick down at any moment.

He ran.

He kicked his legs and pumped his arms and could see his legs beneath him once again and, as he looked onwards towards the finish line, he felt the swish of the tail miss him by inches. There was a crowd of people gathered at the line now: his entire family, and old friends he had not seen for an age. And they were screaming for him.

A quick glance back showed he'd widened the gap slightly. He found some extra speed and let himself feel hope. He knew it was dangerous to do so, but it was his lifeline right now. Another over-the-shoulder glance; thirty yards separated them. Jack felt lighter and stronger, as though he was leaving every ounce of pain and all the baggage that had held him back for decades on that trail. He was about ten metres from the finish line and quickly glanced behind one last time to find the dark predator was now even further back, tired and beaten.

Only yards from the line, Jack felt the pain in his shoulder. It started as a dull ache but quickly surged across his entire upper body, giving him the feeling that he was being ripped in half. He collapsed to the ground, clutching his chest as he felt an invisible force pressing on his ribcage. As the darkness began to sweep over him, one thought popped into his head before he finally lost consciousness.

That would have been a personal best.

Number Seventy-Two

As I reach for the towel, the phone's loud and unwelcome tone rings from somewhere in the house. Thankfully, it's only allowed to ring twice. But suddenly I am distracted by a different noise, a sobbing coming from next door's garden. It's Tom.

Our elevated single storey block provides exceptional views of the bay, but it also means we're privy to the neighbour's goings-on. The bathroom window looks directly into their back yard, and it's like a portal into a reality show but without the pretence for the cameras: a suburban opera of laughter, screaming, shouting, and crying. Nobody stays, and when the final curtain falls and the house goes back on the market, Liz and I are never surprised. There have been bad times, but this has been our home for thirty years now. We have raised two children in this house.

Carefully stepping back behind the peeling frame of the open sash window, I lean close and try and decipher his morose mumblings, but through the tears and croaking, any lucidity is lost. Carefully, I stretch my neck just enough to be able to see him sitting on the white stone seat that he and Susan frequently share throughout the warm summer evenings. But it's October now; the air has a bite, and he must be cold in that T-shirt. It also occurs to me that I've never seen Tom sitting on that seat by himself.

Many people have lived at Number Seventy-two, but they never stayed long. I feel silly saying it, but I believe the house is evil, that something menacing lives there, too, and like a mould spreading its spores, everyone that inhales it seems to turn bad. Too many strange things have occurred: an abnormal number of dead pets, too many heart attacks, depression, drugs, divorce. The list goes on.

Tom gets up and moves out of my line of sight. Only flashes of his white T-shirt are now visible through the sprawling bushes that leak over our side of the fence. But when I hear the raucous sound of metal on concrete, I guess that he's just picked up the spade, the one I saw him using yesterday to prepare the vegetable patch. They've been talking about growing their own vegetables for the last couple of years. Yesterday he shouted across the driveway that he was finally ready. And he winked.

Even the friendliest people seem to self-destruct in that house. Take the last couple, Tony and Melissa. We even got an invite to the wedding. Their positivity was infectious in the beginning, but then the arguments started. The usual stuff, old material that Liz and I have covered many times before: finances, kids, work, and life balance, and so on. Then the accusations came, and through the open bathroom window we heard it all: the screaming and the shouting, the worst names under the sun being bellowed, windows smashed, doors slammed, plates thrown. And the tears. So many tears. I saw Melissa the day before she stabbed him, walking around the garden, cigarette held in a shaky hand, face swollen, and one eye almost shut. I am pleased to say the wedding never happened, but sad they became another casualty of that house.

We loved Tom and Susan immediately and have spent many drunken nights in each other's company. It's the longest anyone has stayed in that house, and we feel honoured to have such beautiful people in our lives. Susan and Liz are like sisters and even started their own book club.

I can still hear him talking to himself but can't make out what he is saying. And then he walks over to the fence line and disappears. Seconds later I see him walking back to the patch of overturned soil carrying four plants. His chatter is becoming more urgent-sounding.

I move my head as close to the window as possible without giving myself away. This time, when he returns to the fence line, he begins to sob. And I can finally understand what he is saying: one word repeated over and over. Sorry.

Suddenly, I feel quite sick, almost lightheaded. It's that bad feeling again, something I haven't experienced since Tom and Susan moved in. I tell myself that it's probably nothing, but this isn't like Tom, not one bit. I hear him sniff and blow his nose and then he's off again with more plants in hand. He stops and looks down at the dark soil. I can no longer hear him, but I can still see him mouthing the word sorry repeatedly.

I shuffle away from the window and poke my head down the hallway. "Liz," I hiss.

I hear him grunting, and it sounds as though he's lifting something heavy. I tiptoe hastily back to the window and see Tom coming back into view, pulling something along. I hold my breath, afraid to give away my presence and watch as the body-shaped bundle wrapped in bin liners and tied with rope is dragged next to the vegetable patch.

My heart begins to thump, and the nauseous feeling returns, but I can't take my eyes away as I watch Tom pick up the spade. He looks directly into our bathroom window, and I immediately drop to the floor.

Three years of festering malevolence.

I stay silent, frozen to the floor.

I'm not sure if he saw me but daren't look back just in case. I crawl away on all fours into the hallway. "Liz!" I hiss again.

There's a frantic knock at the door.

"Brian," Susan's voice explodes down the corridor. Behind her, I can see the silhouette of Tom with the spade.

I see the note on the kitchen table. Liz's handwriting:

Gone next door to get a book from Susan. Back soon x

Face the Music

Max tongues around the gum, willing his tooth to give up the battle, pushing it back and forth continuously, but the tissue shows no sign of giving up. His mum said today was the day, that if it hadn't fallen out, she would rip it out when he got home. And now there is only half a mile to go.

There it is, a hundred metres away. The straw monster, otherwise known as a scarecrow. His tongue begins to flick in and out of the hole even faster as he looks down at the crisp winter soil and ups his tempo to a fast walk. His friend Tommy said he wouldn't take the shortcut for a million dollars—even mid-summer—but especially not December. "Fear is in the mind." At least, that's what his dad tells him.

It's just straw.

There's a sudden icy blast on the back of his neck, and he can't help but notice the accompanying flutter of the tweed jacket and scarf in the wind, and how it cruelly animates the foreboding figure that stands between him and home. The fear feels real enough, and it's getting closer all the time.

The gum feels tender now, and his tongue keeps scratching against the coarse bottom edge of the tooth, but he feels it's a necessary coping mechanism. The wisps of breath are becoming more frequent, and his bravery is dwindling. An involuntary shudder rattles down his spine, and he's already regretting the decision to cross the field for the sake of an extra fifteen minutes—and to impress Tommy. He had a point to prove, and his friend's awe-struck face was a picture when he veered off towards the private sign.

Panic sets in, and suddenly it seems the light is fading impossibly quickly. He wants to be home, regardless of what's in store. This is no place for a kid.

The eyes are in sight now, polished lumps of coal that Max immediately associates with being bad—courtesy of his mum and pre-Christmas threats. A thick red line, possibly painted, is splashed underneath but is too straight to be a smile. On top of the grey fabric-covered head and secured with string is a black velvet hat which resembles one of those found in a cheap fancy witch's costume. Wrapped around its neck is a grey scarf with a single knot in the middle. The jacket covers a white holey vest with some of the straw poking through, and it's tucked into a pair of green pants that look old and half-mast. But the shoes look brand new.

The wind induces trickery once again, and the ensemble begins to sway.

As he approaches the closest point, he begins to edge as near to the barbed wire as possible. Soon he will be within twenty metres of the scarecrow. The lights of the estate twinkle in the background with the promise of his parents, warmth, and food, but it all seems too far away. And then the music begins, eerily distant, but audible, and he realises it's coming from the direction of the straw monster. The tune is familiar, perhaps a nursery rhyme, but the hollow tinny music sends shivers down his spine.

He speeds up. Enough is enough. Another gust of wind and the haunting music intensifies. The monster is once again brought to life and, for a fleeting moment, Max thinks he sees the thick red line twisting into a mocking smile. He looks away quickly but becomes even more terrified when it's out of eyeshot. As he turns back, he swears the black eyes are closer than they were before. Level with the monster now, his legs are kicking as fast as they can, and his heart is thumping in his chest.

The music emanating from the scarecrow suddenly stops, but the silence is not comforting.

He digs his tongue into the sharpness of the tooth as if to focus, and it's then that he feels the tissue break. As the sharp taste of blood begins to fill his mouth, he moves the tooth to the side of his mouth and bites down hard to avoid swallowing it while running. His eyes are becoming watery, and all he can think about is the welcome mat outside of their front door. Past the scarecrow now, he affords a look back but regrets it immediately as he sees the scarf still flapping in the absence of any breeze. He gives in and begins to sob, out of his depth, and longing for the mundanity of being home in front of the television. Eyes forward and focussing on the welcome sight of the hole in the fence, he crunches down on the tooth and runs as fast as he can, but suddenly he is flying as his foot catches the protruding rock and he slams headfirst into the soil.

The music starts again.

He turns around, and the straw monster is undoubtedly closer than it should be. Both ends of the thick red line are curled upwards; the smile is undeniable. The tinny melody speeds up, and Max cannot believe his eyes as the scarecrow shakes itself free from its cross and begins its slow march towards him. Spitting out mouthfuls of dirt, he kicks at the ground for leverage, and a bolt of pain bolt soars up his right ankle. Biting at his lip, he grimaces and finally manages to push himself up.

The music gives way to a raucous mishmash of metallic clangs—the perfect soundtrack to a walking straw demon—and Max freezes in fear. He watches it lurch closer in its shiny black shoes, and he can hear the thick pieces of straw bristling against each other and the occasional soft squeak. It's almost hypnotic.

Finally, he begins to back away and turns and hobbles towards the hole, his tongue nervously threading in and out of the gap in his teeth, the earthy taste of dirt at the back of his throat. Adrenaline kicks in and he starts to run—the pain is getting more bearable—and suddenly he's sprinting again. Glancing back over his shoulder, he sees the scarecrow bending down and scratching around the soil. Eyes forward again, he watches the ground disappear beneath him, and once he feels at a safe distance, he looks back again to see the monster back in its original place. And he knows he is going to be okay.

Already he feels less cold, as though the glow of the nearby halogen streetlights is providing tangible warmth. And soon the smell of cooking dinners wafts into his nostrils. Nearly home.

There is still an expectation that the haunting music will start once again, but then he reaches the wire fence and soon he is clambering through the gap and onto the long grass.

Made it!

A flash of bravery—almost smugness—flows through him as he slots his fingers through the chain-links to look back at the musical straw monster. Aside from the occasional flap of the jacket and flutter of the scarf, normality has returned. He continues to stare into the field for some time, wondering if anyone else has ever been chased through a field by a scarecrow. And then he finally whispers "Goodbye," before joining the pavement and basking in the blue glow of the televisions that emanates from every house down the street.

He laughs as he steps onto the welcome mat, unable to recall ever being so pleased to arrive at his front doorstep. As he swings the door open, the heat immediately envelops him, and the smell of cooking fills him with immense relief.

"Now then, tiger," his dad calls out from the living room.

But right now it's his mum that he needs, and he follows his nose to the kitchen to find her removing pizzas from the oven.

"Good timing, champ," she says. "Now let me look at that tooth."

"It's gone, Mum. I tripped over on the way home, and it fell out somewhere."

"I'm not sure I believe you, let me take a look," she says after slamming the oven door.

And then he begins to cry, overwhelmed with the relief of being back on home soil. He wraps his arms around his mum with sheer joy, and for a while, neither of them speaks.

"What's wrong, love?" she finally asks.

"Nothing. I'm just tired."

They eat their food and retire to the living room to watch some second-rate crime show.

And he feels so pleased to be home.

Usually, a few minutes in, boredom would get the better of him, and he would go and play in his room. But tonight he's enjoying the tedious comforting chatter of his parents. He catches his mum looking at him, and she smiles and mouths, "Are you okay?" and he nods and smiles back.

He watches his dad take a swig of beer as his mum gets back to carefully painting her nails. He thinks about telling them what happened, but it all seems so silly and distant now, like the remnants of a bad dream.

He looks at the clock and counts the minutes until bedtime, the prospect of sleep already filling him with dread. *Thirty-three, that's a full episode.*

There will be no short-cut tomorrow—or ever again, for that matter—he decides. And for the next thirty minutes, he reminds himself of that while he nervously alternates between glancing at the clock and pretending to enjoy the show.

Too quickly, the credits begin to roll and his mum looks at him with *that* look. He nods reluctantly and, after giving them both longer than average hugs, flicks on the landing light and trudges up the stairs to the bathroom.

After carefully brushing around the missing molar, he stretches his lip back with his index finger to reveal the gap. Somewhere in that field is his missing tooth, but the straw monster can keep it. He can already feel his other growing through and besides, his mum will still put the money under his pillow.

With his bedroom door slightly ajar, the sound of the television is just audible enough to be comforting but not loud enough to keep him awake. He jumps into bed and closes his eyes, but all he can think about are those black eyes and how the scarecrow released itself from its cross, then smiled and began to walk towards him. Trying to distract himself from the day's events, he starts to recite each of the presents on his Christmas wish list. Finally, he closes his eyes and hopes for a dream-free sleep.

The sound of his teeth grinding together is almost unbearable, but he can't stop. He's aware of what is happening, but there's a compulsion to keep going. He applies more pressure by crunching and sliding them against each other, and bits are starting to powder off—he can feel them—like the mouthful of gritty soil from the farm. But the teeth continue to break down further, and he can feel the sharp fragments swimming around in his saliva. He doesn't relent but continues to grind, and some of the larger pieces are carving into his gum. As he swallows, he can taste the bitterness of blood and feel the sharp pain of broken teeth lodging in his throat. He begins to choke and sits up with his hands around his neck. He is gasping for air.

And suddenly there is no pain. And no broken teeth in his mouth.

He runs his tongue across his teeth, and they're all back apart from the one he lost in the field. His heart feels like it's going to rip out of his chest and the sheets are soaked with sweat—at least he hopes that's what it is. *It was just a dream. Jesus Christ!*

The television isn't audible and the landing lights are off, which means his parents are most likely already asleep. His heart sinks a little at the realisation. The feeling of being alone is amplified even further when he hears the same faint but undeniable metallic tune he heard in the field, only this time it's coming from somewhere in the house. His chest immediately tightens and a wave of nausea sweeps over him.

"Mum! Dad!" his voice is shaky, but they should be able to hear it with his door ajar. As soon as he gently places one foot on the carpet and peels back the covers, he sees the trail of straw leading from his bed into the hallway. "Mum! Dad!" he cries with much more desperation and conviction this time. But only the unpleasant chimes of the music can be heard. There is no comforting reply from his parents and no sound of footsteps approaching.

He pinches his leg, but already knows it isn't a dream. There is the usual creak of the floor as he puts his other foot down, but one that sounds much more ominous under the circumstances. Being careful to step around the straw, he strides across to the light switch and flicks it on, but the greyness remains. In desperation, he tries it numerous times before finally giving up and nervously swinging the door open. Instantly, the music gets louder, and Max's eyes follow the trail of straw that continues down the hallway and leads to the half-open door of his parent's room.

"Mum, wake up, please!"

His eyes are getting used to the greyness, but that does not counter the looming sense of dread. The music doesn't help. It is louder and carries ominously down the corridor.

Every nerve ending feels raw. In a very horrible way, he has never felt this alive before. There is still no reply from the room, but he considers the fact they may still be asleep. He begins to tiptoe towards the open door and, for a moment, he thinks he sees something move at the end of the hallway—he freezes and holds his breath. *Get a grip, Max.* Finally, he exhales and takes a step forward. And then another. He checks behind him quickly, half expecting the straw monster to be standing there with its menacing smile. And then forward again, step by step, until he is outside the door. Pausing briefly, he takes a deep breath before nervously nudging it open and eyeing the trail that ends at the foot of his parent's bed. Relief floods him when he sees the two bodies under the duvet, and he rushes across to his mum's bedside—and the knot in his stomach explodes. He can't breathe, the room is spinning.

This must be another nightmare. But he doesn't wake up, and he can still see the two straw heads resting on the pillows. Panicking, he frantically rips the duvet off only to find their bodies have also been completely cocooned in straw. Only their eyes are visible, but vacant, glass-like.

He desperately tries to prise the straw away, but it's too tightly wrapped. He begins to sob as he flails helplessly at the mummified versions of his parents and suddenly he is hyperventilating; everything feels as though it's going to wash away in a sea of grey. He reaches out for the bed for balance, but he can't bear the sight of the straw bodies any longer. He runs back into the hallway and leans against the wall, sucking in as much air as possible. And then he makes his way towards the stairs. All the time, the music is getting louder and his panic grows.

His only plan is to run to the neighbour's house. They'll know what to do—Greg and Susan—they'll sort this out. But when he gets to the front door, he sees the two miniature straw dolls nailed to the top frame. On the floor in front of the door is the source of the music: a dull silver music box. In the centre of the box is a waltzing scarecrow dressed as the straw monster was: shiny black boots, tweed jacket, and grey scarf—even the black eyes and thick red smile.

The music suddenly begins to distort, replaced with the grinding sound of metal teeth scraping together. It's beginning to sound like someone speaking, looping incoherently, until finally—and impossibly—the voice lucidly says, "Bring me the tooth now, or they both die," before it momentarily distorts back to the music and finally falls silent.

The snivelling tears come again, and he isn't proud, but he can't stop them escalating into a full-blown sob. Suddenly he no longer feels like a nearly thirteen-year-old. "I don't even have the tooth," he rasps.

He looks over to the box again and notices the tiny drawer in its left side. Afraid the music might begin again or, even worse, that the sinister mechanical voice might emanate once more, he nervously edges towards it and crouches down. Surprisingly heavy for something so small, he gently gives the box a quick shake—and the rattle is instant. Reluctantly, he opens the drawer slowly and reveals the missing tooth, still tarnished by soil and a tinge of redness on the underside. He grabs the tooth and places it in his pocket.

"This is my fault," he yells.

Wiping the tears away from his swollen eyes, he angrily marches towards the front door and swings it open. He continues the bravado towards the field and all that it has in store. But "Fear is in the mind," so everything will turn out okay.

No breeze tonight, just an iciness that bites at his bare feet and through his pyjamas. Only the streetlights illuminate the way; no artificial glow from inside people's homes to indicate signs of so-called life. He is on his own. A million thoughts and fears prey on his little flurry of bravery as he walks determinedly towards the hole in the fence. It's not going to have his parents, no way. *It's just straw.*

Wrapping his fingers around the cold wire of the fence, he sees his new nemesis: no signs of animation, just a dark blur on the landscape. Taking a deep breath, he pushes himself through the fence, and solemnly makes his way towards the centre of the field. He searches for the tooth in his pocket, and for a minute can't find it. Beginning to panic, he pushes his hand deeper. Finally, his fingers brush against its sharpness, and he pushes it into his thigh to take the focus away from his fear, a trick he used at the dentist's. But terror has embedded itself and won't be fooled this time. His shivers are too violent to be put down to the cold alone.

He thinks about turning back and running to the neighbour's house or calling the police, but the monster has his parents. Only ten metres between them now—the scarecrow still inanimate. Five metres, but still nothing. Finally, he stands right in front of it and cranes his neck to look up towards the big black eyes and the even red line that runs across one side of the fabric to the other. Behind the head and arms, he notices the burn marks that run along the edges of the wooden cross, and for a moment he thinks he can smell smoke.

Face to face with the straw monster, he reaches inside his pocket and wraps his fingers around the tooth. Slowly, he brings it out and extends his arm. And then uncurls his hand.

The head snaps down immediately, and the black eyes are looking directly at him. Max lets out a single croaky scream, his bravery departed. Its smile returns and the individual pieces of straw that make up the body begin to slither around each other like snakes. Some of them start to sneak over the neck of the vest and others through the bottom of the pants. The arms are sending out feelers of their own, dry tendrils that dance through the air towards him. For a moment, he can't move and can only watch as the straw monster comes to life. The knot in his stomach has returned, and his mouth feels dry. He tries to take a step back but immediately feels resistance and, looking down, he sees the straw coiling around his legs and snaking slowly upwards. Simultaneously, the straw from the scarecrow's upper half starts to work around his midriff, and he feels the pressure as it slithers up his chest and begins to twist around his throat. He tries to wrestle free, but it's too late. His arms are next as the straw works its way from his wrists and up the entirety of his arm to the shoulder blade. Soon he is cocooned from head to toe; only his eyes spared. He tries to scream again, but it's muffled and becomes even more strained when the straw begins to enter through his mouth, forcing its way down his throat. He's starting to lose consciousness, but he can still feel his arms being raised upwards until he's in the shape of the cross. As the world continues to slip away, he can feel and hear the straw as it occupies him. And then one final jolt.

***

He saw his parents a few days later. It brought them here with no other reason, he supposes, than to mock him.

"What are we doing here, Max?" his mum had said. And that hurt, using his name to address the stranger who'd stolen his body.

His dad came up so close—within a few feet— and Max was so glad to see him again, albeit briefly. The smell of his familiar aftershave made Max ache to be held by him once more. In his father's eyes, there was a noticeable sadness. Max could tell that something wasn't right with him. His mum had the same look of despondency, too. She smiled at the new twelve-year-old version of him, and held his hand, and even laughed once, but he was sure there was an underlying estrangement with the entity. They were living with a stranger, after all.

But then they left and he had to watch his parents walk away. And the knot he used to get in his stomach manifested again, but in much more physical form as he felt the straw in his chest intertwine tightly. The stranger came back that same afternoon and placed the tiny straw dolls and the music box in the pocket of the tweed jacket. "Hang in there," it said and winked before turning and walking away.

His senses have sharpened over the last few days. He can hear the distant noise of children laughing, and music playing—all the nostalgic sounds of beautiful suburbia. His sense of smell is even more fine-tuned: home cooked dinners, perfume, and most recently, blood. Oh, yes, he can smell it on them, hear it pumping around their bodies, and he thirsts for it more and more as each dusk comes.

When night falls, the need is relentless.

He nearly managed to get one arm off the cross yesterday evening, and tonight he will try again.

There is something else, too. His memories are fading and slowly being replaced with other people's, undoubtedly ones that have been trapped inside this straw prison. He has seen each of their deaths and the darkness that accompanies them when reborn, their souls tarnished beyond recognition, eaten away by evil. And he can feel the darkness taking over.

He has seen a lot through the visions, enough to know for the exchange to work, he must be on the cross at the time and his victim must approach him. It is the cross that allows such devilry. He has seen that in the visions, too. It was over three centuries ago that her body was set on fire—nothing left but ashes and the stubborn charred cross—or so they thought, but the witch's curse survived, and he knows it continues to live on through her victims.

The field is his home for now, his world—his prison. To break outside of its confines, he will need a connection, something incredibly powerful that will guide him across to the other side. A piece of clothing might be enough, saliva on the rim of a bottle could work, even a drop of blood on the soil. A tooth would be a billion to one longshot.

Through the barbed wire, he sees the children walking home from school. Sometimes he even sees Tommy. He hopes that one of them will one day soon be brave enough to take the short cut.

About the Author

After a 30-year hiatus, Mark recently gave up a lucrative career in sales to pursue his dream of being a writer. His passion and belief have resulted in pieces in many prestigious magazines, including Flash Fiction Magazine, Raconteur, Breaking Rules Publishing, Books N' Pieces, Artpost, Colp, The Horror Zine, Antipodean SF, Page & Spine, Twenty-Two Twenty-Eight, and Montreal Writes. His work has also appeared twice on The No Sleep Podcast and is set to feature shortly on The Grey Rooms and Centropic Oracle. Seven anthologies to date include his work, two of which are on the 2019 Horror Writers Association recommended list, and a further eight anthologies set for imminent release also contain his work.

Mark resides in Melbourne, Australia with his wife and two children.

https://twitter.com/MarkTowsey12
https://www.facebook.com/mark.towse.75

ALL THINGS THAT MATTER PRESS

FOR MORE INFORMATION ON TITLES AVAILABLE FROM
ALL THINGS THAT MATTER PRESS, GO TO
http://allthingsthatmatterpress.com

Made in the USA
Columbia, SC
20 February 2020

88164702R00098